CW00664058

KAGEROU DAZE

VOLUME 7: FROM THE DARKNESS

JIN (SHIZEN NO TEKI-P)
ILLUSTRATED BY SIDU

YEN ON

NEW YORK

KAGEROU DAZE, Volume 7
JIN (Shizen no Teki-P)

Translation by Kevin Gifford
Cover art by SIDU

This book is a work of fiction. Names, characters, places, and incidents are the product of the author's imagination or are used fictitiously. Any resemblance to actual events, locales, or persons, living or dead, is coincidental.

KAGEROU DAZE VII -from the darkness-
©KAGEROU PROJECT/1st PLACE

First published in Japan in 2016 by KADOKAWA CORPORATION, Tokyo.

English translation rights arranged with KADOKAWA
CORPORATION, Tokyo, through Tuttle-Mori Agency, Inc., Tokyo.

English translation © 2017 by Yen Press, LLC

Yen Press, LLC supports the right to free expression and the value of copyright. The purpose of copyright is to encourage writers and artists to produce the creative works that enrich our culture.

The scanning, uploading, and distribution of this book without permission is a theft of the author's intellectual property. If you would like permission to use material from the book (other than for review purposes), please contact the publisher. Thank you for your support of the author's rights.

Yen On
1290 Avenue of the Americas
New York, NY 10104

Visit us at yenpress.com
facebook.com/yenpress
twitter.com/yenpress
yenpress.tumblr.com
instagram.com/yenpress

First Yen On Edition: July 2017

Yen On is an imprint of Yen Press, LLC.
The Yen On name and logo are trademarks of Yen Press, LLC.

The publisher is not responsible for websites (or their content) that are not owned by the publisher.

Library of Congress Cataloging-in-Publication Data
Names: Jin, 1990– author. | SIDU, 1993– illustrator. | Gifford, Kevin, translator.
Title: Kagerou daze. Volume 7, From the Darkness / JIN (Shizen no Teki-P) ; illustrated by SIDU ; translation by Kevin Gifford.
Other titles: From the Darkness
Description: First Yen On edition. | New York, NY : Yen On, 2017.
Identifiers: LCCN 2015297341 | ISBN 9780316259477 (v. 1 : pbk.) |
    ISBN 9780316342049 (v. 2 : pbk.) | ISBN 9780316308755 (v. 3 : pbk.) |
    ISBN 9780316308762 (v. 4 : pbk.) | ISBN 9780316545280 (v. 5 : pbk.) |
    ISBN 9780316466646 (v. 6 : pbk.) | ISBN 9780316439640 (v. 7 : pbk.) |
Subjects: | CYAC: Teenagers—Japan—Fiction. | Ability—Fiction. | BISAC: FICTION /
Science Fiction / General.
Classification: LCC PZ7.1.J55 Kag 2015 | DDC [Fic]—dc23
LC record available at https://lccn.loc.gov/2015297341

ISBNs: 978-0-316-43964-0 (paperback)
       978-0-316-51243-5 (ebook)

3 5 7 9 10 8 6 4 2

LSC-C

Printed in the United States of America

CONTENTS

CHILDREN RECORD SIDE -NO. 1- (1)

...It's cold. Like I'm lying on top of a freezing sheet of ice?

There was no telling how much time had passed since something had hit the left side of my chest. But I could still see—see the gun pointed at me.

Oh, right. That must have been what got me. That was why I had fallen to the floor. Which means I don't have much time left, do I?

But...Shintaro. What had happened to him? With that injury, he was nearly unsalvageable, right?

...Though, I wonder about that. If it could happen, it might just have happened to him, too. Maybe.

However...this was probably it for me. I was lucky to have made it this long in life, anyway. It'd be stupid to expect a miracle to occur twice.

...Someone's yelling something. It's echoing too much to make out very much, but..."Marie"? Is that what they're saying?

My ears are failing me already, aren't they? And I had just bought that new set of earbuds, too.

I had been looking forward to the TV shows I had recorded, to the movie I was going to see this weekend...But I suppose there was no point now.

It'd be nice if these guys could get out safe, at least.

Not that escaping right now would change their fates at all. But having that thing, that monster, just do whatever it wanted with them...That was just too awful to imagine.

My vision began to fade. His twisted laugh curved and warped in the air.

Ah, my vision's already going. There's no time left. Isn't there some final thing I can do here?

...Wait a second. I feel like I'm forgetting something.

What was it? I couldn't shake the feeling that, long ago, somewhere along the line, I had made this really important promise.

*Oh, right. My power...*What was the first thing I made disappear with it?

C'mon, Tsubomi Kido, think. What did I...What did you see on that day?

Trace your memories.
Back to that day, to that time...

BLANKMIND WORDS 1

"You just love music, don't you, Tsubomi? You're always listening to it."

…Yeah. I do love it, pretty much.

"You know, there was a time when I'd go up onstage and sing, actually. That's right—your own mother! It was just a tiny little stage, but, ooh…it still gave me such a rush. The people who showed up would cheer for me to the beat of the song and everything. Have you ever thought about being a singer when you grow up, Tsubomi?"

…No, nothing like that. I just like listening to it.

"Ah, right, right. Well, so do I, trust me on that one. I totally understand."

…You're disappointed in me, aren't you? I saw it on your face just now.

"Oh, of course I'm not disappointed! I'm just really happy that you and I have something we both like, Tsubomi. Even back when you were still a baby, I've always thought it'd be nice if we could talk about our favorite songs with each other later on."

…Oh. Okay.

"Say, Tsubomi? How about we go to some kind of concert soon? Even if it's the same tune, hearing it in a club—with all the volume and stuff—it can feel completely different! I bet you'd enjoy that a lot. Huh…?"

——No, Mom. It's not like that.

What I "like" is different from how you're using the word "like," Mom. It could be anyone singing, any kind of lyrics…It doesn't matter. I just listen to music because once I have the earphones on and am playing it, I don't get hung up about all the other stuff. Like all the noisy traffic outside. Like your tired-looking face. Like the hospital. It all stops being worrisome.

When I close my eyes and let my body drift into the music, it feels like I'm becoming invisible...mixing into the sound. I really like that feeling. Like I'm in a world with nobody there—not even me—and it's completely calming.

So you don't have to look so happy about it, Mom, okay? I'm not, like, making your dream come true or anything. I'm not the kind of girl you think I am, and I can't do a single thing you're hoping from me, anyway.

...Ugh. I gotta open my eyes and wake up soon.
Well, see you later, Mom. Sleep well.

I had melted into the lightly swaying sea of sound. The melody was like waves lapping, taking me someplace devoid of purpose or meaning. I couldn't imagine how nice it'd be if I ever reached that destination. Forgetting everything. Even losing myself.

The image of my mother from a time gone by disappeared into the waves. I watched silently as it went away, taking with it past memories I had never really been able to express in words.

BLANKMIND WORDS 2

Suddenly, my mind focused on the blurred sunlight on the other side of my eyelids. I opened my eyes and blinked a few times, as the senses in my previously sleeping body gradually stirred and awoke. That body, afloat and bobbing among the soothing waves of sound like a clear plastic bag, slowly regained its plodding weight—forcing me to feel the full shape of my form as it remained sunken in bed.

"Oh man," I said, lowering my eyebrows. "I wish I could've slept a little longer." But it was too late. I was a light sleeper to begin with. In a state like this, I had no way of making a return to that realm.

Resigned to my fate, I removed my earbuds. My ears were relieved of the pressure, and gradually blood flow returned. Turning off the music, I lay there while my eardrums were instead rattled by all the "sounds" that composed the real world. The hateful, blunt, pounding sounds of the outside world.

I sighed and propped up my heavy body. In the hopelessly ornate full-length mirror placed in front of me, I could see an equally extravagant canopy bed reflected back. The bleary-eyed, worn-out-looking person seated in the middle of it looked into the image.

"...Morning."

The image's mouth moved in tandem with mine.

Another odious morning began.

I stretched out my arms and looked toward the window. The bright, cheerful light of spring was working its way through the flowers of the dogwood tree outside, displaying a constant flicker. There was still a crispness in the air, but this tree always bloomed early, and it was showing signs of going into full flower soon. The wavering light-pink petals brought the term "delicate flower" to mind.

Delicate flower. Truthfully, I liked the way the words sounded, but I had always associated a negative image with the phrase. If anything, it provoked me to anger a little.

*   *   *

My name was "Tsubomi." It was a word that, in Japanese, referred to a flower bud that hadn't bloomed. I once asked my mom why she used a word like that for my name. I think she had said it was because "it's a sign of all the potential you have—the potential to grow into your own delicate flower."

I suppose a normal girl would jump up and down and shout, "Wow! That's such a cute name! Thank you, Mother!" And that was how everyone reacted whenever they heard my name. Every single one. They always said, "What a lovely name that is" or whatever.

A word that the entire world loved. Delicate and filled with potential.

"...And what the hell's so delicate about *you*?"

The image in the mirror defiantly glowered with a half-asleep glare. This was no budding flower. If anything, it was more like some kind of noxious weed. There was nothing at all about the name Tsubomi that suited me. Every time someone called me that, I felt like they were sneering. Like, "What's so cute and bud-like about *you*, huh?"

I hated to say it to my mom, but to be honest, there wasn't much about the name that I liked.

As my mind filled with gloom, I could see delicate little Tsubomi in the mirror clouding up her face in tandem, expression as dim as a burned-out bulb. I decided to finally get out of bed.

Putting on the slippers I had thrown off to the side the previous night, I began to walk toward the door. The place was fully air-conditioned—a comfortable temperature, not too warm. I trod along the carpet, decorated with symbolic patterns of some kind or another, and just as I almost reached the door, I heard knocking sounds.

"Ee...?!"

I instinctively let out a languid yelp, wholly unprepared. It wasn't hot in that room, but I felt an uncomfortable sweat begin to form across my whole body.

My mind began to race. Mentally diagnosing how to correctly handle the knock, I immediately opened my mouth. And kept it there. It stayed open...But no matter what, I just couldn't get the words to come out.

"You're awake, aren't you, Tsubomi? If you're awake, why don't you answer me?"

It was a cold, ringing voice on the other side of the door, as meticulously crafted as a high-quality obi, and it had strength behind it. I froze, like a frog in the sights of a snake.

No doubt about it. *She* was on the other side. I'd have to give the correct words in response, or...or...

But the more I thought about it, the more my mind began to jumble. Time passed.

"...All right, I'm opening up," the voice said curtly as the door whirled open. There was my older sister, Rin Kido, the owner of the voice that froze me. Her hair, which had a little red to it, was tied back, her back straight up as she stood there. This early in the morning, and yet her posture didn't reveal a single weakness.

Rin in Japanese could mean "dignified," but also "cold" and "bitter," and I didn't think anyone had ever been given a more suitable name. She was great at everything—intelligent, beautiful, physically active. Nobody in this nation bore the name Rin better.

And here was this girl with a killer case of bed head, fresh from putting herself on the same level as weeds, trying to make her mouth work.

"Uhh...hhmmm...good, good mor..."

My sister sighed at the barely comprehensible syllables I uttered, forehead wrinkling in a show of pity, I assumed.

"Tsubomi, you know I'm not here to try to scare you or anything, okay?"

I knew that, of course. I knew she wasn't the kind of person to get off on scaring me, and I also knew why that graceful face of hers was

pouting at me. But even though I did, I just couldn't connect my head to my mouth. No matter the reason, I just couldn't say more than: "Yes. Yes, I do."

Rin sharpened her eyes further. "Keeping quiet like that," she growled, "you're acting like some grass by the roadside, Tsubomi."

Her words struck me like a knife. My frozen body gradually began to shake.

It was…difficult to speak in general. The doctor said there wasn't anything wrong with my head or vocal cords or whatever, and I instinctively knew that already. If I was alone, in my room, I could chatter on with abandon. It was only when I was trying to talk to someone else that the words petered out on me.

Up until recently, I could still handle it. If someone wished me a good morning, I could wish them one back. Giving basic yes-or-no replies was never any kind of problem.

The reason it had gotten this bad was simple: One day, at the children's center my mom took me to, I was with a boy who started making fun of my speech. That was the start of it. I don't think anything he said was particularly cruel or abusive, either. The grown-ups around us didn't see it as worth dwelling on, quickly ordering the boy to apologize so we could all drop the subject.

But no matter how much time passed, I couldn't let it go.

Right up until that time, that moment, I had never considered what my voice and word choices sounded like. As a result, the meaning behind what the boy told me came as an incredibly heavy blow. It meant that, compared with other people, there was something weird about me. The instant that thought crossed my mind, it was like someone had turned out all the lights in my head.

Back on that day, when the full meaning became clear, I ignored all the grown-ups around me and started punching the boy. That wound up becoming the bigger deal to them. My mom kept bowing in apology to that kid's parents for the next several visits afterward.

*   *   *

After that, I started avoiding situations that involved talking, and now I was so timid about it I couldn't even communicate simple words or concepts.

"...All right," said Rin, crossing her arms at me from her hallway position as she grew more impatient. "It's fine." Then she set foot in the room.

Great. I did it again. If I don't respond to anything she asks—not a single question—well, that'd make anyone angry. I lowered my eyes, unable to take the strain. The shadows from the dogwood blossoms were creating undulating patterns on the carpet. Even in silhouette, they were as delicate as always.

...It was just driving me crazy. My voice, my name, everything.

What kind of hopes did my mom used to have for my future? Or maybe all those dreams were now focused on sharp-minded, strong-willed Rin instead.

But I'd never know how she really felt. You can't ask a dead woman a question and expect an answer...And I mean, even if Mom were still alive, I couldn't speak a single word. I couldn't even "ask" her anything.

How many words had I even exchanged with my mother since that episode—back in that cramped apartment we were in?

No. I haven't changed at all since then. It's going to be this way for the rest of my life. I know it will. There was no way I could ever become the delicate flower my mom was hoping for.

Thinking about that, about how pathetic and useless I was, made the inside corners of my eyes start to heat up.

My sister's feet approached, trampling over the dogwood silhouettes. I stared at her. She already had one arm in the air.

I winced and shut my eyes, expecting a slap. But the pain never registered across my cheek. Instead, I felt something soft brushing down my disheveled hair from the top. Surprised by this, I suddenly opened my eyes and looked at Rin again. She wasn't smiling, but she didn't seem to be angry, either. She was just staring down at me resolutely.

What was weird about this was that she was patting me on the head and definitely *not* slapping me on the cheek. Maybe this was a new way of expressing anger that I wasn't familiar with, but either way, this behavior was new and confusing.

Then Rin slowly parted her lips and spoke.

"Bread or rice? Which one do you want?"

...Bread or rice? I was more of a rice person. It went with a lot more food than bread did, and I liked how it tasted. But why was she asking me that now? Not to put too fine a point on it, but the general flow of things had indicated she was about to scream her lungs out. Something along the lines of "You're gonna stay in your room until you tell me why you're not answering me" or whatever. I would understand that. But why's she asking me about my starch preferences...?

"Ah...," I exclaimed out loud. An idea came to mind. It never showed up when it'd actually be useful, but my voice would always find its way out when I surprised myself over something. It was so mean.

Rin betrayed zero reaction to this. She stared at me, apparently waiting for a reply. I shivered a little.

"Bread" or "rice"...She must have meant those terms to mean some kind of punishment. That would explain a lot of things. I had seen crazed murderers on TV shows offering their victims a choice of deaths to experience. And it was all too easy to picture Rin as capable of something similar. She might have used harmless words like "bread" and "rice," but that only made it all the scarier.

If those *were* punishments, it was easy to imagine them as cruel and/or painful. My imagination began to go wild. What would "bread" mean? Was she going to sandwich me in something, or use the toaster oven as some kind of torture device? It was a bit tougher to figure out "rice"—a rice cooker didn't seem too well suited for physically tormenting someone—but already I felt horrified.

Which answer would be better to give? If I said something like "I don't want either," would she fire back with "Okay, noodles, then" or something—and then, oh God, stick my hand in boiling water, or...?

Maybe I better pick bread, then. No, wait, rice...

"Tsubomi?"

"R...r...*rice*, please!"

Being called by name made my mouth reflexively spit out "rice." At pretty high volume, no less. Loud enough to startle Rin a little, by the looks of it, but I was even more shocked. It might very well have been the loudest I had ever shouted, since I was born.

The blood began to pump hard into my skull. I had gone from one extreme act of rudeness to another. It was all over. "Rice" might not be enough to punish me with anymore. I was starting to picture the potential introduction of *fried* rice to the menu. Boiled up, and left in the wok to simmer.

As my mind zoomed down ever more ridiculous pathways, Rin's resolved gaze suddenly melted into a smile. I didn't know why that happened, but—as inappropriate as it was—I caught myself thinking, "Man, she really *is* beautiful."

Rin gave my head a few pats with her outstretched hand, then bent down, bringing her eyes to mine. "All right," she said. "I'll try to whip up something really great for you today." Her voice had all the sharp tones it came with by default, but it still bore a sense of warmth that seemed to permeate my skin.

Ah, what do I have to do to start speaking like this? I couldn't help but admire her.

Having had her say, my sister turned around on her heels and lightly padded off. I stood there silently for a little while, then started freaking out again. Maybe "something really great" meant the level of punishment in store. Little else crossed my mind as I got dressed and headed for the breakfast table.

Even during the meal, Rin acted like she was on cloud nine. My dad's work had apparently been going well, to the point where we were talking about how they might expand into new businesses, so maybe that's what she was happy about.

I remained prepared for my slaughter the rest of the day, but at the end of it, I reached nightfall without any sort of rice-related punishment. Kicking my slippers off, I burrowed into bed and stuck my earbuds in. It was only then that I realized the rice served with breakfast that morning had been noticeably tastier than usual.

I've never made the mistake of thinking too highly of myself, but I had no idea I was *this* much of an idiot.

I was always good at test taking. I was in the ninety-*something*th percentile in the national college test-prep exams we took at school. That's why my dumb sister used to ask me for help on a lot of things. She'd always say, "Come *onnn*, Big Bro" like the impertinent little sister she is. I'd always take the hard-line approach, trying my best to offer her guidance. It's not like I had any other choice, after all.

All of this should have been enough of a sign that I wasn't so dim-witted. And that's not all. There was this girl who dyed her hair brown and joined one of the higher-level cliques in class, and one time she told me, "You're, like, super-smart, Shintaro." Hee-hee, fond memories.

…No, wait, hang on. I messed up. Now I remember: I replied something like "Nrr…rpphh…" to her, didn't I? I barely got out of bed for a while after that. Crap. That's a shitty memory, then, isn't it? Better forget all about it.

Regardless. I think, or like to think, that my mind somewhat resembles the proverbial steel trap. I can gain a grasp of most concepts after having it explained once, and I was usually good at retaining that knowledge. Brainy. A *brainiac*, even.

But something was starting to distress this beautiful mind. I was faced with a bit of a tricky situation…No. Not a bit of one. A pretty tricky one. A super, incredible, doomsday-level tricky one.

Two in the morning on August 17.

Underneath a dimly luminescent bulb, the living room of the Mekakushi-dan's hideout was laden with a somber, oppressive atmosphere. We were face-to-face with one another, surrounded by an assortment of tacky toys and weird statues from countries I couldn't venture a guess on naming. To an eyewitness, it might have looked like a meeting of high priests for some New Age cult.

Though maybe that wasn't so far from the truth. This was the

Mekakushi-dan, after all—unusual characters, supernatural abilities, no real rules in place. In terms of its creepster aspect, it ranked right up there with your run-of-the-mill cult.

It was Kido, leader of the group and one of the four members left in the living room, who cut through the tension first. "So," she said, eyes swiveling between the others as she kept her voice low, "anyone got any last words?"

Her stare settled on Kano, her most common target for abuse and whining so far that day. His shoulders shivered a little.

"Well, uh…heh-heh…not really."

The usual easy-breezy smile on his face was gone. In fact, he was now white as a sheet and sweating profusely. I felt bad for him, but what could I do? I was honestly a little mad at him myself, besides.

I mean, we've all got a skeleton or two in our closets, I supposed. Or, in my case, a hidden folder on my computer. Or two. Or five. It might actually be in the double digits by now.

So yeah, a dozen skeletons or so.

But.

Transforming yourself into other people's friends and family and acting like the real thing? That's kind of hard to swallow.

It all began late last night, when he turned into Momo and started provoking me. The real Momo didn't seem too shocked or concerned by Kano's little coming-out party, but I wasn't much of a fan, to say the least. And what brother would want to see someone besides his sister doing God knows what while pretending to be her? No brother *I* know.

And then it turns out he had been long-term prodding me as Ayano, exactly as she looked on that day two years ago. When Kano sprang *that* on me, well…It was rough. What she said back then made it impossible for me to so much as go outside. I've been obsessing about it ever since—it's driven me to suicidal thoughts several times.

Those were the kinds of games Kano was playing with me. And if the past couple of days encompassed strictly those two experiences,

I'd probably never want to see the guy again. It'd give me enough depression fuel to keep the engine running for the rest of my life.

But—another but—he then opened up about everything with me. It turns out, from that day two years ago up to the present, Kano had been running around the city doing whatever he could to rescue Ayano. He had had that monkey on his back ever since we were all in high school, and I never even noticed.

And assuming that's true, then what Kano told me in Ayano form—about how it was my fault for never noticing anything—well, it was actually pretty darn true, wasn't it? There wasn't a single thing wrong about that accusation. I failed to notice any aspect of Ayano and what she was caught up in.

And knowing that your own father was being infected by some freaky monster that was putting your own siblings and school friends in danger…I wondered how that made Ayano feel. Maybe, in all the inane conversations we had, she was dropping little hints. Hints I could've seen as the pleas for help they undoubtedly were, if I was paying attention. But I didn't. They went in one ear and out the other.

…The regret was hard to grapple with. If we had noticed something, anything, maybe she'd still be with us. And not over *there*, in the other world: the Kagerou Daze that swallowed her up.

The sight of Kano quivering like a fruity dessert under Kido's withering gaze apparently blunted her appetite for further violent outbursts against him; she sighed and hung her head. Indeed, her feelings were no doubt mixed as well—some of the people she'd spent much of her life with had been hiding earth-shattering secrets from her. It might have been too much for her to swallow at once.

Kano looked on worriedly as Kido's eyes fell to the floor. It wasn't hard to guess his feelings on the subject. It was about more than not wanting people to be angry at him. It was a huge, impossible-to-picture sense of desperation that he had shouldered solo for two years, all for the family in his life he wanted to protect. He was probably afraid he created an equally large helping of despair for Kido just now.

Everyone has a secret or two. Most people, though, keep the secrets in order to protect themselves. This one, on the other hand… He wasn't thinking about himself at all there. All those feelings he must have had for his sister, for his family…all while he was going toe-to-toe with a reality that must've made him want to pluck his eyes out.

Kido raised her head back up. If she was going to continue with her mental games against Kano, I was just about ready to mediate between the two. I didn't have to worry.

"…You could've told me sooner, you idiot," she drawled out in a monotone. "We're family." Then she sank back into the sofa and fell silent.

Kano looked ready to cry for a moment in response but seemed to catch himself just in time. "I totally will next time," he bashfully replied.

The "supernatural" occurrences they…well, *we*…were dealing with probably weren't the kind of thing we could tackle very easily. It came with a presupposition of our collective deaths, for one. The ensuing dread wasn't fun to deal with, and for now, we had contrived exactly zero ideas for avoiding that fate.

But seeing these family members interact with one another up close made me think of something. The way they discussed secrets, accepted them, and still joined hands and faced forward. *That* was the real strength of the Mekakushi-dan. They were struggling with fate, and unfairness—two incredibly powerful foes—and the strength they brought to the battle wasn't fading at all.

Even if this was an enemy none of us could handle alone,

something told me we already had the best weapons in the world to deal with it.

...Eesh. It can be a bit socially awkward, hanging out with them like this, but they really *do* make a good brother and sister, don't they? Kano certainly seemed apologetic enough about it, and I had no great desire to bring up the topic again. After all, we had a mountain of problems to solve that was starting to stack up to Everest-size proportions. And we really needed to get to the main issue soon, or else time was going to be tight...

...As I was thinking this, from the corner of my eye I spotted a quivering shape with long black hair begin to stir. *Whoa, whoa, what's she standing up for? She's not gonna run on us, is she?*

As expected, *she* edged her way toward the front door, robbing the room's atmosphere of whatever family togetherness we had just created.

"Hey, where, where're you going?" I said to the girl's back. She stopped just as she attempted to complete her ninja-like escape. She had her very long hair in a pair of casual ponytails, and the hoodie she had borrowed from Kido billowed around her stomach, apparently much too large a fit.

"Oh, um...the bathroom," she replied with an awkward smile as she tried to deflect our gazes.

"You just went about ten minutes ago," Kido countered. "Is your bladder that tiny or something?"

The girl struggled for another excuse for a few more seconds but wordlessly gave up and threw herself back down on the sofa with a *whump*, facing me. She was Takane Enomoto, the second defendant of the day—presently turning away from me with the exact same attitude and surliness she had exhibited two years ago.

"Okay," she began, "so did we, like, have something else to talk about, or...?"

It seemed like I could hear the blood vessels around my right temple explode at the get-me-out-of-here demeanor that oozed from every pore in her body.

"Oh, okay. So you think that's all the explanation you needed to give for the year of shame and self-loathing I experienced at your hands...?"

"Pfft," Enomoto replied at my resentful jab. "Shame? *You're* always the one putting it on yourself, isn't it? Bitching about 'Oh, please don't look at these porn vids that I've scattered around my hard drive like candy' and stuff. Oh, which one did you watch a lot of lately? I think it was something like 'Teen Foot-Fetish Frenzy, Part—'"

Oh, look. Promptly going for the jugular again. The Fetish Protection Safety Valve in my brain immediately issued a warning. Sweat oozed out from my own pores. I needed to close the book on this, and fast. So I leaped off my seat.

"What?! You...You're one of those...Um...Privacy! Yes! All right? Privacy!"

...Silence.

I could tell without looking at them. Kido's cold gaze was already gouging my right cheek. Kano, still regretful about our previous conversation, didn't try to laugh it off like he usually did; instead he gave me an expressionless stare. He was *totally* using his ability, too. I could feel it.

Enomoto, meanwhile, giggled. An evil, familiar-sounding giggle it was, at that. She plainly still loved pushing all my buttons as she tried hiding her smile with one of the hoodie's large sleeves. Oh God, they *totally* looked alike...that little gesture both of them did. I had no idea how I went a year without noticing. If I could go back in time, I'd tell my past self to take a hammer to all my electronic devices and go camp out in a mountain shack instead.

"Yeah," she gleefully continued, "well, I'm not the one who tried to play this cool and *sooo* above-it-all character in school, with *those* fetishes you had. Like, I was seriously shocked! What a total piece of work you are..."

"God damn it...!"

There was something hideous about the way Enomoto wallowed

in her malice. I gritted my teeth and tried to calm my mind—every synapse seemed ready to burst with rage. God damn it, indeed. I wasn't expecting *her* to show up at this point. And with the absolute *last* outfit and appearance I wanted to see her in, too…!

She had appeared several hours earlier, dropping in with a casual "Yo" as I was seated on the sofa, still tired from our earlier impromptu mountain hike.

We had a "frenemies"-type thing going at the time—she was the only classmate of my friend Haruka—so we couldn't help but see each other fairly often, because she was pretty much glued to him the entire year. They'd eat lunch together, and sometimes I saw them hanging out at the arcade during off days. There was no way either of us would describe ourselves as "friends," but…All right, she wasn't a terrible person. Back then.

It was definitely her, after all, that gave the closest and most ready support to Haruka when he needed it. He needed it a lot, around that time. And sure, she was rude, crude, mean-looking, and always ready to shoot you down a peg for no reason apart from assuaging her demonic personal gratification—but with Haruka in the picture, I was willing enough to accept her presence.

That was then, of course. Now it was vividly clear to me how easy I was being with her, how wrong I truly was. I thought she was some kind of devil-spawn at the time, but that didn't go nearly far enough. No, this was an arch-demon, the kind that would make even the most gifted of the late-night infomercial psychics run screaming in their bare, anklet-laden feet. She was, after all, the woman hiding behind Ene, the evil spirit that had just wrapped up a year-long torment session with my mind.

I mean, why did this have to happen? And why to me? What did I ever do? If there was some kind of election to vote for the last person in the world you wanted to share a secret with, I'd buy up every ballot so I could vote for Takane Enomoto. Maybe Kano, too, if I had some extras.

But again, no point in dwelling on it or creating elaborate fantasy revenge scenarios. Enomoto already had a grasp of every possible weakness I boasted in life, and she wasn't afraid to give them a little squeezy-squeeze whenever she wanted. I was helpless.

But—no, seriously, why? Is God dead or something?!!

Enomoto, for her part, looked extremely proud with that corrupt, despicable smirk still on her face. She had put me on the defensive so far, but I wasn't about to go down without a fight. Even I had some tools to work with; after all, over that whole year when "Ene" was building up her war chest of material to use against me, I was right there on the other side of the screen.

"Well, look," I began, making the effort to enunciate every syllable in my declaration of war, "you can say whatever you want, Enomoto, but don't you think you're kinda forgetting something? Like how you introduced yourself as 'Ene, your regular neighborhood computer girl'? Or how you kept on calling me 'master'? 'Ooh, master, master...' You haven't forgotten *that*, have you?"

The reaction, as I thought it would be, was immediate. "Uh," Enomoto groaned pathetically, before covering her face with both hands and crumpling to the ground. It was a ghastly sight to see.

"That," she continued to moan, "that...I was just, like, feeling out my abilities, seeing what I could do, and...and it got me all excited and stuff, and...uh..."

She was having trouble breathing. I moved in for the kill.

"Oh *really*? So all that time, you were picturing yourself as this darling little tomboy flying around in my computer? Is that really the mental picture you had in that dismal, gossip-obsessed brain of yours? Man, talk about degenerate."

"Aaaagghhh!!" Enomoto screamed as if I'd just cast a spirit-dispeller card on her forehead. The way she reared back, edging away from me, made me feel like I was running an exorcism—and why not? She was the devil herself! She deserved to be banished! Returned to the world she belonged in!

*   *   *

As we engaged in this farce, the door flew open behind me. "You're too loud!" Marie griped at us. "What time do you think it is right now?!"

Everyone on the scene froze, staring in her direction.

"At least turn out the lights when you go to bed," she grumbled before closing the door.

...I had been in this situation before. You stay overnight at a friend's place, you screw around for too long past bedtime, and a mom comes storming up the stairs. You could never argue with a grown-up like that, and at somewhere well past a century old, Marie sure had us beat on age.

Enomoto and I shared glances, grimaced, then extended a hand to each other in almost perfect synchronization.

"...Let's just forget about it, Shintaro."

"...Sure."

We shook hands, both of them still wet with sweat, and forged the armistice.

...Wait. No, we didn't. Her eyes aren't smiling at all. She's planning to kill me once I let my guard down. I'll need to sleep with the door locked for a little while.

Based on what she said, Enomoto apparently made contact with the Kagerou Daze on that day two years ago. The results turned her into Ene, and I guess she must've obtained either the "awakening eyes" or "focusing eyes" ability Azami mentioned in her diary. Turning invisible or shapeshifting or whatnot was easy enough to comprehend, but Enomoto's skill was a little tougher to interpret. Basically, she removed her consciousness from her body and could take it pretty much wherever she wanted. She couldn't manifest "Ene," her spirit-self, in the real world, but otherwise it sounded a bit like an out-of-body experience.

It was every bit like she was an evil spirit—which would've suited her perfectly. As Kano put it, "Each ability has its likes and dislikes when it comes to 'vessels,'" and that was a perfect example if I ever saw one.

Once Enomoto obtained that skill, she had been flitting around all the electronic networks of the world, in search of the physical body she lost when the Kagerou Daze got her. That, as she put it, led her to my computer.

I lowered myself, sinking deeply into the sofa, and brought my voice back down a few notches. "But why did you come to *me*?" I asked. "You must've had someplace else you could've messed around in."

Enomoto frowned. "Well, not really. I mean, Haruka was dead, and Ayano wasn't around, either." She looked at me. "Plus, it kinda seemed like you were gonna die if I left you alone, so…"

"Uh…"

Now we were at the crux of the issue. I hated her for getting right at it like that. But I couldn't just brush it off.

"…Yeah, I'm not gonna deny that," I replied. "What with Haruka and Ayano gone, I…You know, I was super-depressed."

It was a good point. By the time this girl showed up as Ene, I was deep in the depths of desperation. I was filled with sadness—having lost two classmates I knew really well—and then Kano disguised himself as Ayano and said…*that* to me. I could never let that go, and it was driving me nuts.

The days after she appeared on my computer desktop were filled with humiliation and disgust, sure…but in a way, I think it saved me a bit. Thanks to her going around like a chicken with her head cut off, I managed to pull myself up and out from that abyss. If she wasn't there, I might've actually gone through with something.

As I remembered this, Enomoto began shaking one of her legs, a nervous tic I hadn't seen before. I looked at her.

"You just said 'what with Haruka and Ayano gone,'" she blurted out. "But, uh, aren't you kinda forgetting someone?"

…Oh. That. Now I knew what was irritating her. I sighed, quietly enough that Enomoto wouldn't notice. Hesitating here would make her snipe at me even more. I decided to just be out with it.

"…Okay, yeah, it was a huge shock when you went away, too, all right? Of course it was. You don't have to make me say it out loud."

"Well, good." That was apparently enough to please her. She let out a big smile, one that didn't look like it matched her face at all. *I swear, the way she engineers every facial expression like that, calculating exactly the response she wants—that's pure Ene.* It was weird how much that struck me right then.

"I just, you know…" She paused. "I'm glad I could actually hear that from you. Because it was kinda feeling like I was in some crazy dream state that whole time, in a way." She put a hand up to her shoulder, bent her legs, and stretched out on the sofa.

"What do you mean?" I asked, not really getting it. This turned Enomoto's smile a bit downward.

"I mean, I was poking around the net that whole time as Ene, but I didn't find anything about *me*. About my disappearance." Her face grayed. "And not just that, either. Haruka's illness, Ayano's suicide, me vanishing…That all happened on the same day, you know? Would people find that weird, usually?"

I hated to admit it, but she was right, and I agreed with her. Like she said, two years ago—on August 15—there were a lot of events that took place in tandem without making much sense. Haruka finally succumbing to his illness was one thing, but Ayano's death? Enomoto disappearing, and all on the same day? That wasn't normal, no matter how you looked at it. People should have been looking for a link…or treating it as a crime, for that matter. And yet there was zilch about it on the news. That *was* weird. I wasn't sure how to respond to that.

"Were you watching the news back then?" Enomoto prodded. "You shut yourself in your room around then, right?"

I wasn't a fan of the way she phrased it, but I shook my head instead of bringing it up. "Yeah, but I didn't do that," I said. "I didn't want to see my dead friends get talked about on TV and stuff. I was too depressed to turn it on, anyway."

"Oh no?" Enomoto responded, pulling back. Why wasn't she gentle like that with me more often?

"...Wait a sec," Kano butted in. "I was watching it back then. Takane's right—it was amazing how nobody ever touched on it at all. Like, it blew my mind while I was watching." Now his own voice deepened, seeking to make an impression. "I think she might be right. Maybe this entire city was already taken over by then. By this...crazy power."

Then we fell silent for a while.

Kano didn't say it to scare us or anything, I don't think, but it seemed to have that effect on Enomoto. *That* was unusual, but maybe she couldn't be blamed. If some "crazy power" did actually exist, it meant that everything we took to be normal in our lives wasn't anything of the sort at all.

Since Enomoto showed no signs of wanting to talk, I decided to pick up the slack. "So you're saying that 'clearing eyes' thing you were talking about is strong enough to wrap an entire city around its finger?"

"I don't mean that, like, it's just really strong or whatever," Kano warned as he reflected a bit. "I just mean that the 'clearing eyes' power that took over our dad had its own sense of will, and that will is what we should *really* be worried about. 'Cause it's incredibly smart...or, like, it's just got this huge amount of knowledge to it, sort of. I'm willing to bet that since it's come to this world, it's been using that 'knowledge' and my dad's body to build up money and power for itself. That's the kind of authority you'd need to take over an entire city."

He shifted the position of his legs under him. "I know it sounds like some kind of joke, but..."

Some kind of joke, huh...? Definitely. There weren't many stories out there as silly as this one.

Kano was saying this super-brainy guy had taken control of every aspect of this city from behind the scenes. If a living encyclopedia like that—a full grasp of everything from the start of civilization up to modern science—actually existed, then maybe Kano's theory had at least a little bit of merit. If this "clearing eyes" thing had the power to take over how everyone and everything worked and even control their hearts and minds, that might just be enough to run an entire city.

But it just made no sense at all. All of us had certain mental borders within our minds that we referred to as "common sense." Accepting anything that went beyond that as some kind of divine given was never going to be easy. But "common sense" was a concept. It wasn't fact. And if the past three days had taught me anything, it was that the values I had associated with "common sense" throughout my life were beyond brittle and weak.

These people with their fantastic "eyes"; this other world separate from our own; this tragedy being set up for us in such exquisite fashion…All these nonsensical events were connecting themselves together and slowly, silently, forming the unassailable "reality" that was now spread before us.

No matter how much I doubted it in my mind, I couldn't do anything about what was being presented. Things had already deviated far from the realm of believing or not believing in it.

"It just makes you wanna laugh," I blurted.

Enomoto's eyebrows arched. "What about that makes you want to laugh? You starting to lose your marbles or something?"

"I'm not losing my marbles, Enomoto. I mean, you and Kano just shocked me, pretty much, and I think I get how much of a bad situation this is. It's just…"

I stopped. I wasn't sure whether it'd be worth saying what came next. If it was the me of any time before yesterday, I probably would've shut down my mind and said never mind. But right then, for some reason, I didn't feel any need to hide my true intentions. I thundered on, not bothering to choose my words carefully.

"This is a lot better for me, you know? A lot better to hear all this, as opposed to when I was holed up in my room not knowing anything. Whether it makes any sense or not, the first step to standing up to something is being able to see it in the first place. I mean, this is a breath of fresh air and…stuff. That's how I feel."

I kind of ran out of steam toward the end, but it seemed like my point had gotten across. "Wow," said Kano, who had listened on silently and now looked slightly relieved. "I'm sure glad we can rely on the new guy here."

Enomoto, on the other hand, had trouble digesting it. "Mmm," she intoned. "Well, I read in the text from Ayano that my teacher was getting all messed up. If it was some kind of ability doing that to him, then it would've happened before any of us even got admitted to that school, right? I guess Mr. Tateyama and Haruka have known each other for a while, and it wasn't until my third year of middle school when my grandfather started suggesting I go to that high school out of nowhere...You think we were all gathered there for our abilities? Then killed off, one by one?"

Her face scrunched up, as if about to cry. She hung her head low.

"I tried not to think about it at all, but...I don't even know what's going on anymore. I don't know what I should believe."

I opened my mouth. I wanted to say something instead of leaving her to dangle there alone. But I couldn't find the words. Kano noticed, perhaps, because he turned to Enomoto in my place.

"I don't wanna sound like I'm defending my family or anything, but I'm pretty sure Dad never even realized he had that skill."

Enomoto tilted her face back up. Her eyes were glassy, like I thought they'd be.

"This skill works by taking your will. Your sense of self, really. I don't think you'd have any memories of when it took you over. So, I mean...I think it's still safe to trust in him. At least, the one you knew in school. That we knew at home."

She bit her lip a little. "Yeah," she whispered as she turned her head back down again. I knew she and Haruka liked and respected Mr. Tateyama as their homeroom teacher—and now the man was standing accused, an alleged murderer. I couldn't even guess how much of a shock that was.

But Enomoto nodded a few times as a sign of reassurance and brought her face up again. Her expression was back to its usual sneer.

"Yeah. He's still a really good guy, I think. I don't mind believing in that. And I really don't think someone like him could've engineered something like this, either. There's nothing all that 'clearing' about how he acts and talks, at all. No...I think it's all that ability's fault."

Then she let out a defiant chuckle, as if releasing something that had festered inside for too long. I didn't follow her logic all that much, but she seemed pretty convinced. I'd take that over depressed Enomoto any day—I could never stand dealing with that again, if I could help it.

"But here's the thing, though," she added. "If this 'clearing' power's carrying out some wild conspiracy like this, then what reason does it have to kill us? If it's already capable of pulling off all this incredible stuff, why can't it just leave us alone and do whatever it wants?"

Kano shrugged and scowled. "Uh...I think I explained that a little bit ago."

"Oh? Well, maybe I heard it, but I didn't really get it."

The two gave each other puzzled looks.

"To create a Medusa," I interjected. "That's what it wants, Kano?"

"Yeah. I am *so* glad you're here right now, Shintaro. Things move along so much faster with you..."

Yeah, thanks. I don't want you to put me on the same intellectual level as Enomoto, if you can help it.

"Yeah, I knew that, but that muh-*doo*-sa thing, like...," she said, proving my point.

According to Azami's diary and everything else we knew, there was a grand total of ten different "eye" abilities. Bringing them all together would be enough to recreate the Medusa race in our modern era, and that, Kano thought, was the aim of our enemy. Apparently, this inevitably meant the death of all the other ability holders.

So those are the stakes. Either we stop the enemy's plans, or everybody in the Mekakushi-dan except me is dead.

It was absolutely crazy, but…

"…We're gonna have to stop this," I said. Enomoto and Kano nodded in unison.

"Well, okay, first things first. We don't have much time left, yeah? If we're gonna stop this thing, we gotta get movin' already."

"Yeah," Kano agreed as he stretched out his body. He reminded me of a cat like that, in some ways. "Whether we like it or not, it's all gonna end tomorrow night. I think if we're gonna have a strategy in place, we better start thinking about it right now."

Looking back over the past few days, I didn't recall him doing anything like stretching out in front of me like that—something that'd leave him defenseless. Letting go of his secret must've helped him relax a little.

Once this is all over, maybe he'll be willing to tell me a little more about the past. About Ayano, about Haruka…and about everything else I didn't know about back then. Once this is all over, anyway.

I exhaled a bit, attempting to tighten up my thought processes as I looked around the room and its members. "Okay," I said. "…Whoa, don't fall asleep. Boss, we need you here."

Kido was just about nodding off. I rubbed her shoulder, and she distractedly opened her eyes. *Eesh.* With her as our leader, we had every reason to fear for our lives…although with the rest of the team, the apples didn't exactly fall far from the tree, either. Everyone in this hideout might have less than twenty-four hours to live, and yet they were barely able to remain conscious.

I turned back to Kano. "Can we get started with our strategy session? If we screw this up, it's game over, people."

Kano grinned at me. "Hey, you're good at games, right, Shintaro? We've got a lot riding on you!"

I took the bait. "Who do you think you're talking to, man? I got the only perfect score in the game your dad made, remember?"

It was, and still remained, a fond memory. *Headphone Actor...* Maybe it was just a sideshow to the rest of the school festival, but it was still pretty enjoyable. I'd give it at least three and a half stars.

Kano snickered and sat up on his seat. "Right on, Shintaro!" he exclaimed, picking up on the newfound energy in the room. "I'm ready to keep this going 'til morning."

When it came to allies on this newfound quest of mine, he was probably the one I could count on the most. He had revealed everything about himself, after all. But I still questioned him somewhat. Looking around, I noticed Kido staring at Enomoto, looking kind of like she wanted to say something but couldn't figure out what.

"Wh-what?" Enomoto finally asked.

"N-no," Kido hurriedly replied, "I was just wondering what you wanted us to call you. 'Enomoto' by itself makes you sound kinda lame."

Lame? Come on. If we're talking about nuances here, what does calling me Shintaro all the time sound like? That's even lamer. Still, I kept myself from blurting it out as I gauged Enomoto, looking slightly bashful.

"Ene's fine," she muttered. "It'd just be a pain in the ass to change it now."

It turns out—and this was news to me—"Ene" was her online handle. Given how her mind worked, it must've been tremendously embarrassing to be referred to as Ene in the real world. But now, it looked like being in the Mekakushi-dan could make anything feel a little bit better.

And so, I took out a pen and began drawing a rough sketch.

Our "enemy" was hiding out someplace that, uh, turned out to be a tad larger than we were expecting. But we didn't think much of it. All these extraordinary events thrust before us had perhaps numbed our ability to feel the true weight of things.

It was an exhausting day overall, but I felt terrific. My second wind must've been blowing in. It was shaping up to be a long night.

*   *   *

The "clearing eyes" that had infiltrated Mr. Tateyama's mind had already infected the entire city, opening its enormous mouth wide to swallow us up. It was probably safe to assume we couldn't trust anyone else anymore. We were facing off against an honest-to-God *monster*—the one who related to Azami how to build the Kagerou Daze. There was no time left for fooling around. If we didn't come up with a way to stop its diabolical scheme, we'd all be this creature's next meal.

…Then, from deep within my mind, I felt something. Something burning, in a way that I had never experienced before.

I thought on it a little, then reflexively grinned. The battle against this shadowy group, the supernatural things happening to us, the monster that appeared, the team that'd come together in response…

"…Holy crap, I'm not the hero of this RPG party, am I?"

I tried not to let my intelligence go to my head too often, but I had the distinct impression I had what it took to drive the despair out of all these people's lives.

Kido had kicked off Operation: Conquer Kagerou Daze thanks to a mixture of excitement and eccentricity. Now, it was a reality.

After all…every one of our lives could be riding on this plan.

Before I was born, my mother was the kind of person you could build an instant rapport with. She tended to take better care of how she looked than a lot of people, which I think helped, but she just had the warmest smile you'd ever seen. I think *that* attracted more people to her than anything else.

I couldn't even imagine how hard it was for her to keep a family going by herself, but—from my perspective, at least—I had never seen her struggle with or complain about anything she did in her life. She was all smiles, she got excited about going on trips like a little kid: She was so lively, all the time.

I'm sure everyone must have loved my mother. A lot of them were crying these big, round tears when they filed past her casket during the ceremony.

The afternoon of that day marked the first time in my life that I'd seen my father. Everyone was crying their eyes out around him, but he didn't shed a single one. All he cared about was what time it was. I still remember how bizarre a sight it was.

According to what I heard from my mom's friends, my father already had a family by the time he met her. He wasn't even aware that I was born until after my mom died. A lot of people were against him taking me in as a result, but one thing no one could complain about was the amount of money in my father's bank account—and so, I found myself sleeping in this room the night of the funeral, flopping around in bed while watching the chandelier above.

I don't really know what my father was thinking, taking me here. The servants who worked here still gave me the cold shoulder, and my father's wife—I guess she was my mother now—was someone I had yet to either meet or talk to.

My sister, Rin, said she had always been the type of woman to stay in her room most of the day—but she was just being nice to me. I didn't tell her about it, but one of the servants told me once that "the lady of the house's health has turned for the worse, in no small part because of you" and that I should "mind my own business."

That was the response I got when I had made a little request. It floored me. It wasn't like I went there because I had wanted to. And that weirdly polite language—"the lady of the house." It made my skin itch every time. Why did every conversation have to be a high-pressure game of wits?

It was clear that people around the house weren't exactly taking a liking to me.

It was July, already over half a year since I had moved in. My daily duties mainly involved reading the books I borrowed from my sister—otherwise, it was a pretty idle life. Nothing to do, no responsibilities. They said I could use the TV in the parlor whenever I wanted, but the thought of running into a servant there squashed that idea.

So there I was, resting my head on a writing desk (a hand-me-down from my father) and wasting time. The afternoon sun must have gotten in my eyes, because I was seized by a sudden urge to move my legs a bit. It wasn't like I ever enjoyed playing outside much, and I was hardly an athlete. But with all these hours spent cooped up, I needed to release my extra energy somehow.

I used my knees to push the heavy antique chair back and headed straight for the door. Not that I was going to run out the door and play some soccer in the park. I didn't really know the local neighborhood, for one, and for two, I was generally forbidden from leaving without permission—I guess the people here didn't like me going out much. By the same token, they'd buy me pretty much anything I asked for, and it wasn't like I had errands to run outside the house, so I didn't see it as any great hardship.

I mean, if I asked them, I'm sure they would've let me go out for a little bit. But running into a servant, in and of itself, was a dreadful, gloomy experience. I could never count on them to lift my spirits.

Besides, there wasn't any reason to hit the park in the first place. It didn't take me long to think of someplace in here with plenty of room for soccer. The Kido manor courtyard. That was how enormous it was. I was all ready to go, my heart quickening as I changed from my slippers to my outdoor shoes and made a beeline for the place, leaving my room behind me.

The afternoon courtyard was, as always, tranquil. The manor surrounded it on all four sides, so to say the least, it was huge. I knew the general layout now, but when I first showed up, I'd get in all kinds of trouble after becoming hopelessly lost.

As Rin put it, my father worked for a "conglomerate," something very ancient and honorable that had been in operation since our great-grandfather's generation. "My grandfather built this mansion sixty years ago," I remember her telling me, nose in the air. It was hard to picture how long sixty years was, but judging by all the furnishings that lined the corridors I had advanced through, I could tell it was a really long time, more or less.

Running to the edge of the upstairs hallway, I instinctively nodded at the portrait of my grandfather hanging on the wall as I headed down the stairway. On the first floor, I was greeted by wine-red carpeting, red enough to give me heartburn, extending the entire length of the hall.

I realized I was starting to get a little sick of this. I was headed for the courtyard to get some exercise, and yet I was already losing my breath?

But I was almost where I wanted to be. *Why don't you run the rest of the way, Tsubomi Kido?*

Let's do this, I thought, as I flexed my Achilles. Then, across the once-quiet hallway, a melody began to echo. There was no natural breath to it. It was delicate and carefree, but something about the stickiness of each tone sounded familiar.

"...A violin?"

As if lured in, I took step after careful step toward the sound. Luckily for me, it seemed to be coming from the courtyard. When I reached it, the door leading outside was already open—no wonder I had heard the music from so far away.

Up close, it was more than just pleasing to the ear—it was practically vivid. The sound of a musical instrument played live was more than just "nice" or "beautiful"; there was a unique sense of vibration, of warping, of the occasional odd note—all mixed together to form true audio timbre for the first time. I never understood the attraction to things like songs and vocals, but the melody of an instrument caught my heart every time.

Just as I was about to curiously poke my head in, I suddenly stopped myself. If I showed up at that moment, I might have interrupted the performance. No, it wouldn't be good to put a damper on things. *Let's just listen to it here for a while*, I thought to myself.

I placed my back against the wall and carefully sat down, trying to be silent. Then I closed my eyes, turned my ears to the melody, and found myself unexpectedly starting to nod off. I tried to restrain myself, picturing what would happen if I let myself fall asleep on the floor there, but the dry summer breeze from the courtyard caused my consciousness to slip away without a fight.

…I wasn't sure how much time had passed. I only felt myself sleeping for the barest of an instant, but when I awoke, everything had changed.

The sound of the violin was gone; the wind blowing in had ceased. *Weird*, I thought as I opened my eyes—only to find Rin giving me a sullen look.

"…That's not very good manners, Tsubomi."

"Agh…!"

Surprised, I tried to stand up on the spot. But I went too fast; my hand slipped against the floor, causing me to sprawl out. I peeled myself off the ground without so much as a groan, and this time I used both hands to get up. As I patted myself down, I looked back at my sister. The sullen look was now one of exasperation.

Not again. I can't believe I did it again. When it comes to making careless blunders around here, I must be some kind of genius.

I opened my mouth to take a breath. At a time like this, I knew I needed to calm down and express exactly what I wanted to say.

"I—I was sleeping…I'm sorry."

The words that came up had a much easier job of finding their way than before.

"Mmm. Well, try not to do it next time."

My sister nodded. She didn't say anything else.

Over the past few months, I guess I'd managed to speak a lot more than I had before. It didn't sound natural, still, but in terms of communicating how I felt, I could do that with just about anybody. I chalked that up to my sister making a heroic effort to speak to me on a daily basis.

Of course, I still made a lot of mistakes. Depending on the nature of my errors, I could get scolded pretty badly. But Rin never took advantage of that to pick on me for no reason—never. And that made me trust in her more than anyone else in the manor.

"Why were you even napping in a place like this, anyway?" My sister raised an eyebrow. "Your bed probably would've been a lot more comfortable."

It wasn't like I fell asleep because the hallway floor was the epitome of plush comfort. I opened my mouth to defend myself.

"I—I was listening to the violin play, and I…just…"

"The violin? I didn't hear anything from my room…Who was playing it?"

I had to keep myself from audibly gasping. I thought it was her—I couldn't picture anyone else. So it wasn't? I was so taken in by the sound that I didn't even bother to check in the courtyard.

"I was just listening to the sound of it, so…uh, I guess I didn't see."

"Well, there's no reason to be sorry. It's fine. But a violin, though… I didn't think anyone in this house could play."

"…Huh?"

I couldn't hold it in this time. If this was someone singing, that set the bar low enough—but a violin wasn't something just anyone could handle. And, of course, I wouldn't know, but would Rin—a member of this family—really be equally in the dark?

"Hmm…It might be *that* again."

My sister crossed her arms and glanced at me, all but demanding a response.

"…'That'?" I replied.

"Ooh, didn't I tell you before, Tsubomi?"

She was putting on airs again, her voice quiet. I started to have a bad feeling, but I just had to know where it was going. I fidgeted a bit.

"Well, I've told you about it, haven't I?" Now she spoke like she was acting in a play. "About the origin of this manor?"

That I knew. The whole sixty-years-old thing. I gave her a nod.

"Ah, well, Japan was a pretty unstable place to live in at the time, but we still built this jumbo-size mansion here, so…let's just say my grandfather kind of stood out a lot. We had burglars come in here on more than a few occasions, looking for valuables."

I pictured the man in my mind. I had only seen him in that portrait. As for the burglars, all I could imagine were the pirates in striped shirts and black eye masks I had seen in children's shows.

"These robberies happened so often, in fact, that they put my grandfather at his wit's end, pretty much. So one day, he finally snapped. Some burglars tried to sneak in here, and he trapped them inside a basement room, right in this manor—right under the hallway we're standing in, in fact."

Rin tapped at the floor with her toes to prove her point. I imagined the round-faced pirates bawling inside a medieval dungeon cell. Her pointing out the location made me take a few steps back.

"B-but that's all in the past, right?"

It was scary to even think of something like that happening here. My sister leaped at the bait.

"Ooh, I don't know. I heard about him trapping those robbers in there, but I never heard anything about him letting them out! And even if I wanted to find out, the key to the basement door's been missing ever since my grandfather's time."

She never heard about them being let out. Which meant they were still in there? There was no way someone could survive for over sixty years in a cage without any food. They'd have to be…

*   *   *

...Wait a second. Is this a scary *story?*

"Uh, um...!"

"Hmm?" Rin's lips curled up a bit.

"Um, i-is this—? This isn't...a good story, is it...?"

"Oh, you don't think so? Aw, it's fine every now and then, don't you think? Why don't I just tell you the rest of it?"

"N-no, no, it's almost dinner, so we should probably..."

I was desperate. I hadn't even looked at a clock, and here I was dragging dinner into this. But what did I care? I had to stop her, immediately.

"Aw, but this story's gotten me so excited and everything! It's just starting to get fun, too, so I really hope you'll want to listen on..."

My lips were shaking. Hers, on the other hand, were smiling, barely containing laughter. *Someone* was enjoying this. So much for never picking on me for no reason. And I had *trusted* her.

I can't stand this. Scary stories were the one thing I couldn't tolerate. It wasn't a matter of being kept up late at night—for someone like me, I wouldn't even sleep the next day.

If I heard the ending to this tale, it'd be all over for me. I did *not* want to be tormented by dreams of criminals tonight and for every night after that. Absolutely not. I was ready to beg her for mercy.

Rin laughed—guffawed, really—at this act on my part before patting me on the head. "Aw, you're such a cute kid," she marveled. "I'm sorry. I was just kidding around. Sure helped you wake up from your nap, though, huh?"

A little bit, yeah. In fact, I may very likely never sleep again for the rest of my life. Thanks a lot, Sis. And the worst of it was that, despite her malicious laughing, I didn't see it as a personality flaw. After a joke like that, it'd just get all awkward if I made it into a big deal. But I did say one thing:

"When I hear a scary story, I can't sleep by myself at night..."

If she started going on with stories like these every day, after all, I'd run away from home before long. I was rewarded with another pat on the head.

"…Though, really," my sister said, "who could that have been? I don't think it's a ghost or anything, but…"

"I—I definitely heard someone playing an instrument. It might've been a TV or something, though…"

If my sister was insisting that nobody here could play, that had to be it. It was hard to imagine someone breaking in just to practice the violin in somebody's courtyard. It seemed natural to assume that someone was playing a recording or something, and I mistook it for the real thing. Maybe the sound was just echoing into the courtyard from someone's room. I still had a bad taste in my mouth about it, but as long as it eliminated the "ghostly violinist" theory, I didn't care.

My sister seemed equally unconvinced, but she uncrossed her arms, apparently seeing no point in arguing. "Well," she reasoned with a haughty sniffle, "maybe one of the servants was playing. It's getting close to dinner, like you said. I'm going back to my room."

I wrinkled my nose. There was the smell of something faintly fragrant in the hallway. I was just trying to change the subject, but I suppose my internal clock hadn't failed me after all.

So I decided to return to my own room as well. I had gone out for some exercise, only to take a nap on the floor instead. I exhaled a sigh the moment the door closed behind me. Every time I tried to do something, it never seemed to work out. I had no idea why.

My legs took me to the bed. I lay down in it, following the wood grain on the columns that held up the canopy as I considered that violin.

Laughing it off as a case of my ears fooling me, I thought, was probably being too hasty. It was a clear, vivid sound that wafted into my ears. I really didn't think it could be anything besides a live performance.

Suddenly, I recalled a time when my mother took me to see a jazz band. I could still remember the moment they started playing—the live energy coming across in sound form, mixed in with the noise from the crowd. It was a feeling that had encompassed the room and everyone in it, something no recording could capture. What I just heard had the same feel to it.

But if Rin was telling the truth, there shouldn't have been anyone in this house who could play violin in the first place. She said it was possible one of the servants had a musical bent, but even if one did, would he or she be playing in the courtyard of the mansion in the middle of the afternoon?

Maybe it *was* someone from outside the manor. Someone who was locked in here, sixty years ago…

"…N-no! No, that's not true!"

I leaped out of bed and shook my head side to side. I had no idea what my brain was doing. Why was I tying the noose for myself?

I was just wrong about what I heard. That's all. That's all it has to be. I was starting to feel helpless as I turned on the light, even though the sun hadn't fully set yet. Still, I wandered around the room as I waited for dinner.

After a while, there was a knock on the door. "Yes?" I said.

My sister peeked in through a crack. "I think we're ready for dinner…Geez, you're still all freaked out?" She grinned. I had no idea how she knew.

"N-no, not really…"

I tried to put on an act. The way I kept my nose pointed squarely at the ground proved to be my downfall.

The second-floor dining room my sister took me to was already occupied by my father, who was sitting down and reading the evening newspaper. He said "Hey" in response to her muted greeting, but the look on his face didn't change a bit. He was never one for tact—really, he was downright unfriendly to people. That would be fine, as long as he had something to say to make up for it, but my father didn't even have that. Basically, you had no way of figuring out what he was thinking.

My sister and I waited silently for dinner to arrive as my father's eyes remained on the newspaper headlines. It was always one of the most difficult things to bear, living here.

After a few minutes, the meal arrived. The main dish was a kind of grilled beef; it came with cooked broccoli and carrots diced in some sauce. *Carrots. Hmm…*

Carrots, huh? Guess I'll have to eat them.

Just as we began eating and I prepared myself to wage mortal battle with my vegetables, my sister spoke up.

"Hey, by the way, Tsubomi said she heard someone playing the violin out in the courtyard. She didn't see who it was, though…Do you have any idea?"

I froze in place, a carrot piece still skewered on my raised fork. *Wait a sec, Sis. You didn't have to ask our father about that, did you? You know he'll just say "Your ears must've been fooling you, kid" or something.* In fact, ever since I had arrived there, I had never seen my father have any kind of palpable reaction to anything.

But despite my expectations, I found his gaze fixed on me.

"…You listen to music?"

The sudden question threw me. It was probably the first time he had ever asked me a question. I looked toward my sister for help, but her face was just as blank—it must have been a rare and novel sight to witness for her, too.

I had to reply, or else who knew *what* would happen. I mustered my mental strength.

"I, um, just a little."

"You *do*…?" my father said, narrowing his eyes before turning to the meat on his plate. "…She listened to it a lot, too, whenever she could."

Before I could comprehend what he meant, I heard a sharp *clink!* coming from my sister's seat. I looked over. The knife she was carrying was now on the table; it must have bounced off a plate on the way there. She was a huge stickler for etiquette, so this was naturally a first. It seemed like she didn't really know what had happened, either, but once she regained her senses, she blurted out a "Sorry about that" and turned her eyes downward.

He must have been talking about my mother. My biological one. I couldn't imagine what else would elicit that disturbed reaction. And why wouldn't it? Talking about a woman who betrayed the both of us, in a way, is a pretty serious affront.

I wondered why he brought it up at all. There was nothing I could read from his cold, indifferent eyes.

But…yeah. I guess that was the case. My sister must have still been in a state of shock over me and my mother. She had been hiding it the whole time as she interacted with me. Maybe she doesn't harbor any good feelings toward me at all. It wouldn't be one bit strange if she thought it'd be a better world without me.

Simply having me around, after all, meant that everything—all of it—was true. If I wasn't here, maybe she could've convinced herself it was all a lie instead.

Thinking about that made my hand begin to shake. I felt nauseated. A bit of a groan escaped my lips.

"Tsu-Tsubomi?"

My sister's worried tone made something explode in me. I shot to my feet and ran out of the room. I could hear something crashing loudly behind me; I must've knocked some of the tableware over. But I didn't turn back. I ran along the hallway, went downstairs, and headed for the front door.

Pushing the heavy door open and bolting outside, I could see the shadow of the front gate lit dimly by a nearby street light. If I was going to escape these walled-off manor grounds, it would have to be through there.

I ran over and tried the bar that ran across the doors. It was padlocked in place and immobile. I looked up to see if climbing was possible, but the sheer height was nothing I could ever manage.

Of course, even if I could climb that thing, what was I gonna do then? If I went away in this awkward state, they might try searching for me. And how would that affect my sister…?

…No. I can't just flee.

The moment the thought crossed my mind, I found myself unable to withstand the nausea. I crumpled to the ground. I tried to put myself together, but even breathing was proving to be a challenge. My vision started to grow bleary, the inside of my head burning in pain.

The cold stone pavement under my palms began to rob me of my body heat. It felt like I was being swallowed up by the darkness of the night. And, ah, if only that could've really happened. If I had no place to live, no place to go, I couldn't imagine how easy it would've been to just disappear on the spot right then.

Yeah. That's right. I should just disappear. Then I wouldn't be a bother to anybody.

Even now, in the dead of summer, the light wind failed to warm my skin. I could always blame my shaking on that. That was easy.

But if I wanted to disappear…I could do that by myself. I knew how simple that was. In fact, I noticed this too late, if anything. *I just have to stay like this, and…*

Suddenly, I felt something heavy on my back. I realized it was my sister's hands, trying to pull me up. I tensed.

"Let—let me go."

"No. I won't let you go. Where do you think you're going at a time like this? …Come on. Let's go back to your room."

There wasn't the usual firmness behind her voice. Her breathing was ragged. I knew she must've run after me. But I just couldn't give the usual obedient reply.

"N-no. Why can't you just leave me alone?"

"I can't do that. I'm your sister. Why wouldn't I be worried about you?"

Your sister. In the eyes of the law, anyway, she was right. But the story behind us wasn't simple enough to wrap up in a single word. Her father ruined his daughter's trust when he created me. Was she truly capable of using a word like "sister" so breezily about me?

I didn't know. I was scared. I violently peeled Rin's hands off and turned toward her.

"But if…if I'm here, then…It's hard for you, isn't it? You keep on thinking about stuff! I…I…I'm the daughter of my mother!"

The words and tears came out like I was coughing up each one. My sister's face, blurred in my vision, seemed half-scared, half-unsure about what to do next.

Why did I have to step up and say things to make her hate me? That was supposed to be the one thing that scared me most.

…But maybe not.

Maybe I was *really* scared of being betrayed by someone I believed in. That's why I wanted them to hate me instead.

It was ridiculous. Trampling all over my sister's kindness for such a ridiculous reason…I was just awful. But this meant she didn't have to get herself worked up over me anymore. There wouldn't be any patting me on the head if I was too hot to touch.

That's what I thought, at least. From the bottom of my heart. Until Rin brought me closer.

"…Who cares about whoever gave birth to you? You're the only sister I have in this world. My favorite."

That was what I heard as she pressed me deeply into her chest. The anxiety and fear silently tumbled away, turning my head into a white blank, nothing left floating in it.

I tried opening my mouth to express my feelings. I wanted to say "I'm so happy" or something, but none of the rushing emotions allowed themselves to be put into words. All I could manage was some weak-kneed sobbing.

I kept it up for a while. Then I shot my head up, realizing that tears, or my runny nose or whatever, was starting to stain Rin's white blouse.

"I…I'm gonna ruin your clothes," I said, even though it was a little too late to warn her. My sister stared blankly at me for a moment, then quickly regained her soft smile and brought my head to her chest.

"Oh, that doesn't matter."

The scent of her hair entered my nostrils. It smelled like orchids, I thought. Pale, beautiful, dignified. It suited her perfectly.

*   *   *

I couldn't help but marvel at it. How beautiful, how strong, and how gentle my sister, Rin Kido, was. *Will I ever be like that someday? Someone so willing to accept others and gently bring them closer to her heart?*

The chilly night wind now felt pleasant against my flushed cheeks. Enjoying my sister's warmth, I kept her hands close until the tears stopped.

When I first entered the industry, my manager taught me a lot about how a pop idol was supposed to act. Whether the camera was on me or not, he said, it was totally important that I conducted myself as though someone was always watching.

"I've been acting that way since elementary school," I replied, a little too cheekily than I should've. My manager smiled. "Wow, you've been carrying yourself like an idol for that long?" he said.

Not that I wanted to. I just had this weird effect on people; I would constantly attract attention, to an honestly scary level.

According to what my brother told me yesterday, this "captivating eyes" ability was one of the supernatural skills that came to people who made contact with this otherworldly phenomenon known as the "Kagerou Daze." Occult stuff like that would normally get me kind of excited, but this "captivating" thing…It was more annoying than anything else.

I wasn't even all that pretty, besides. And yet, just walking down the street, I'd have strangers chasing after me who'd erupt into cheers if I spoke even a word to them. Cameras would go off all around me, no matter where I was. It had been going on ever since I was a little kid, so being obsessed over how people saw me was an everyday thing for years.

Thus, when it came to acting "like somebody was always watching," I was confident that I was a lot more sensitive to that than your average pop star.

…But now, I've started to give some more thought to my manager's words. He said to act like I was being watched. He didn't say "A lot of people will be watching you, so be prepared for that." I suppose what he was trying to get at was "Never forget that you're an idol at all times, in all places."

By that definition, I was a total washout. I had two servings of the *katsudon* rice bowl our boss cooked up last night—it's her specialty—and after running around for the entire day, I'd found myself falling asleep on the sofa for the second night in a row. I didn't even wake up until after noon today. Not too many people—women, especially—are capable of sleeping on a stranger's sofa in their living room, I don't think.

It wasn't like anyone tried to wake me up, either. In fact, Seto and Marie had to eat breakfast while huddled away from me, all sprawled out on the sofa. I wonder how they did it.

…Though, hell. That problem didn't have anything to do with being an idol in the first place. I could just die, I swear.

All the silly crap I did today was enough to astonish even Shintaro: "You've gone way past freaky and full circle back to amazing," he told me. That might be the first time he's ever complimented me, actually. Heh-heh; I want to die.

So now, this *katsudon*-obsessed pop star is in a bit of a fix. More than a fix actually. A crisis, maybe? Or maybe a world-shattering impasse. Yeah. That's what I was facing.

It was 11:50 at night, and a lukewarm wind was blowing on my face. The moon was hidden under thick cloud cover, the bare street lamps and passing headlights from cars the only things illuminating the paved roads.

We had walked maybe half an hour since leaving the hideout. Conversation was sparse as we plodded along silently before arriving at the front gate of our target point—the "enemy" base.

"…Are you kidding me?" Hibiya shivered. "We're gonna break into *that* scary building?"

Behind the high walls was a gigantic Western-style structure, a shiny black color in the darkness. It loomed above the gate, and like Hibiya said, it was the textbook definition of "creepy." If this really was the enemy's hideout, the foreboding gloom it exuded certainly made it look the part.

But it was still a bit hard to swallow. I mean, the building wasn't meant for any inherently scary purpose.

*　　*　　*

It was the main building of my high school.

Two years ago, right before Shintaro was first admitted, the school underwent a pretty large-scale renovation.

You'd think "renovation" just involved patching up the broken or worn-out parts of the building, but by the time they were done, it didn't seem like a renovation. More like a complete rebuild.

The building itself was fully redone, of course. There was also a strong, durable wall built around the surrounding land, complete with an electronic security system. I don't know if the "enemy" my brother talked about had planned all that out, but it was certainly one reason I was willing to believe his tale.

I still remembered what it was like when work began, for one. I passed by that battered old schoolhouse all the time—then one day, construction started, and in the wink of an eye, it was transformed into this. Looking back, they certainly wrapped up the project in lightning speed.

It was right around that time, in fact, that all sorts of new buildings began to get built in the neighborhood. That was something I got to experience for myself, and I couldn't deny that my brother's theory—that that's when our enemy began to hatch its scheme—sounded awfully correct.

"Wow," I stubbornly countered, "it sure gives you a different impression from the daytime, huh...? You aren't scared of creepy stuff like this, are you, Hibiya?"

Hibiya gave me an exasperated look.

"Oh, come *on*. I'm just saying, it's creepy because we don't know what's inside. I don't believe in ghosts or anything...but what about *you*, Momo?"

"Mmm, I'm not really affected by any of that stuff. Oh, but Shintaro and the boss are total pushovers! We went to a haunted house a bit ago, and she actually fainted in there."

"Whoa! What?" Hibiya's eyes lit up as he grinned. "That's kind of a surprise. She acts so chill all the time. Guess not so much in real life, huh?"

I was kind of the one who made her faint, by the way...but I wasn't exactly lying, either, and there was no point in going into the nitty-gritty. The boss didn't seem to remember, anyway.

That was the sort of pointless conversation we had as we waited for the appointed hour. There didn't seem to be anyone there, in the school, standing around blithely in the middle of the darkness. Come to think of it, today was supposed to be the first day of remedial lessons after the Obon holiday; I wound up cutting class in the end. There should've been people going in and out for club activities, but there was no activity.

...Hmm. I'm still not sure I totally get this. What was this "enemy" of ours thinking, building his den of evil underneath a public building? I took another look around but naturally failed to find any answers from my vantage point.

"Do you think the school's really...the hideout and all? I'm having trouble believing it."

"I'm not too sure this 'enemy' of ours even exists, for that matter," Hibiya added. "You go to this school, right, Momo? You didn't notice anything?"

I shook my head. "Nothing. Like, if I did, I'm sure everyone else would've, too, and then it'd be a huge deal."

"Ooh, you never know, though," he replied, still on the alert. "Like, maybe this evil organization's already brainwashed you and stuff."

It sounded like something out of a children's superhero show. Something told me that if any "evil organization" existed in this town, we were likely it. The "Mekakushi-dan" wasn't what any decent, upstanding group named itself.

"Nah, I doubt it. I don't think any of the students here noticed anything up with the school itself. I mean, I didn't."

"Yeah, but the way Shintaro put it, this 'enemy'...It's your teacher, right? The one who took us to the park yesterday?"

I had difficulty forming an answer. As if noticing the silence, the wind chose that moment to begin gusting.

I knew it in my head, and I didn't mean to cast doubt on my own brother. But to be honest, I still didn't entirely believe everything

Shintaro said. That someone's after us and our "eye" abilities; that this entire city's already been taken over by some sinister presence; and most of all, that the diabolical mastermind behind all this was Mr. Tateyama, my homeroom teacher.

When I first heard that today, I was pretty much speechless. If Shintaro hadn't been the one to say it, I don't think I'd have believed one bit of it. But that's exactly what he said. He was never a totally reliable presence in my life, but I knew he was smarter than pretty much anybody, and I knew he wouldn't spout off a bunch of BS during a crisis like this. Never.

He had to be telling the truth, and I had absolutely no rationale for thinking he wasn't. So I didn't want to call it a pack of lies…But still, it came as a huge shock. I think I would've felt a bit better about it if I could've talked to Shintaro some more. But he acted all broody about something or other, so I couldn't even do that.

My mind, uncaring about my feelings, began to conjure up all kinds of worst-case scenarios. I grew anxious that all these amazing, irreplaceable things I'd encountered over the past few days would fly away, never to be seen again. It made my chest feel like it was about to cave in.

Really, if there was a God out there, he could be a real prankster sometimes. Why were we being asked to put up with all this? I never asked for anything unreasonable, I didn't think. I just wanted a *normal* life. One where I could be with everyone else. That was it.

"…Momo?"

Hibiya's voice flung me back to reality, while his right hand was tugging at the hem of my hoodie. The anxiety on his face a moment ago was gone, and his cheeks were puffed out a little bit. I must've been too slow to respond for his tastes.

"Umm…," I said, trying to pull my mind back together.

"Look, if you're worried about something, just say it. Do you really trust me that little?"

"…Huhhh?" I was bewildered.

"I mean, I'm nervous, too, but...like, we gotta do this, don't we? We all talked it out together—get it all back and put an end to this. If you're gonna act all nervous about this...you're gonna start messing me up, too, all right?"

Then he turned around, a bit ashamed of what he'd just said.

The wind, making a boisterous noise until now, had calmed. We were enclosed in silence.

"Uh...thanks. I...I'll try my best."

I was just too simple like that sometimes. Listening to Hibiya was all it took for the anxiety that filled my heart to cower down and hide in the shadows.

Which is fine, I supposed. *It's fine, but...I don't know.* The creeping feeling that was expanding in its place wasn't any less comfortable. *Kids these days...They sure know how to keep it together! Um...Ha-ha-ha. Oh, brother.*

"Aaall right!" a blunt voice shouted. "Sorry to interrupt you when things're getting heated, but it's just about time to move!"

I followed the voice. It was coming from my pocket. Taking it out, I was greeted with the image of a girl with twin ponytails, glaring at me and looking extremely peeved for some reason.

"Ah...Ene?! Since when were *you* in there?!"

"Oh, since the 'Thanks, I'll try my best' part, I guess?" she replied, a mischievous smirk on her face. Reflexively, I applied pressure to both sides of the phone. The screen began to creak.

"Aaagh!" Ene shouted in response. "Wh-what're you doing?! If you break this phone, the whole operation's gonna fall apart! All of it!"

She spread her hands wide to prove her point. The time display above her read 11:55 p.m.

"Well, that's your fault for sneaking up on me, Ene. Ugh...So did Shintaro and the rest get inside?"

"You bet they did! Ha! I bet they didn't expect me to break into this security in ten billion years! I had the entire thing busted wide open in seconds! It's stripped down to the bone!"

Ene stood tall in the phone, arms crossed. I was amazed that she could keep that tension going even at a time like this. It was really like, like she's…

"Well, good job, Ene. I'm glad we can count on you."

Ene froze for a second, not expecting my praise, before beaming from one end of the screen to the other. "Yeah, totally! I'm just, like, a fiend, aren't I?!"

Hibiya, looking on from the side, hefted a long sigh, as if there was nothing more for him to comment on. "C'mon, Momo," he said. "We gotta get started. You know what you're supposed to do?"

"Umm, probably!" I replied with a smile. Hibiya nervously tensed up his face, the way he always did.

I was trying to act the clown for him a bit, but of *course* I knew my role in all this. With Ene's consummate security-breaking skills, the entire school was now ours to explore. Assuming everything was proceeding as planned, the other group was using a map drawn from Hibiya's ability to march right into the central core of our "enemy's" hideout.

But, as Ene warned us, "once they notice the security's offline, there's no telling what kind of dudes they'll send in from the outside." We had the lock open, in other words, but we might have some company soon that didn't approve of it. At all. They could very well be armed, too, and given the Mekakushi-dan's lack of sophisticated battle training, we wouldn't last long then. And as long as we didn't know how much of this town was really in the grasp of our enemy, there was no counting on any external support.

…*But that's where I come in.*

It was now three minutes to midnight. My mission was just about to kick off.

Ene must've known as well. "I spread the word on the net that you're here right now, like we planned," she told me, showing some rare seriousness for a change. "You pop idols are somethin' else. You wouldn't believe how nuts people are right now."

Straining my ears a little, I could already here the murmurings of faraway people among the sounds of the night. I retired from the industry for pretty personal reasons, but tonight, I might just have a chance to make up for it.

"Thanks, Ene," I said.

Ene grinned. "Hey, we're all friends here! No need to hold back now!"

I answered with a smile of my own. Then I handed the phone to Hibiya and turned back toward the school gate.

Looking back, the last time I had set foot in here was...*OH. Just three days ago, huh? It feels like forever at this point.*

Three days ago, I was headed here in a total funk, ready to kick off my remedial courses. I never imagined summer school would turn out this way—joining the Mekakushi-dan, running into all these people, encountering something like this...

It was starting to feel, by now, like I was completely detached from reality.

"...Hey, Momo? Can I ask you something?"

When I turned around, I found Hibiya staring me down, something clearly on his mind. Then it struck me: This could very well be the last time we were ever in the same place. I nodded back to him.

"You're, like, this incredible idol, right, Momo? I—I think that's the whole reason I came here in the first place. You're probably the celebrity Hiyori wanted to get an autograph from."

Hiyori. The girl Hibiya came to town with. The one who was probably suffering in the Kagerou Daze right now. Someone Hibiya had to rescue at all costs.

"So, uh, when this is all over...can I get an autograph?"

I had somewhat mixed feelings about this request. One, assuming we were successful at all, it meant I was permanently retired from the pop-star business. An autograph from someone like me wouldn't make her excited much at all.

Two…I dunno. I guess I was a little jealous of her. That kind of thing.
But before I could answer, Hibiya continued in a half shout,
half sob:

"So…swear we'll meet again, all right?! Promise me!"
…*Promise, huh? Fair enough.*
"…Sure. I promise."

We went through the gate. A familiar sight greeted me as we
briskly walked onto the school grounds. As we did, I thought over
things one more time. The last time I was there, in the midst of my
epic moping session, I found myself looking up to "normal" teens
getting to actually live out their golden years. Now though, as I
walked along, I felt like I was there. That I was finally doing it.

There was none of the bright sunlight I basked in on that day, but
there, standing in the middle of school grounds, I bet I was shining
just as brightly.

The sounds of people I just barely heard in the wind earlier were
now perfectly clear in the air. I could tell that my pulse was quickening at the noise. It was the first time Shintaro tasked me with such a
major role before. I had to give this everything I had.
Taking a deep breath, I focused. Already, I could feel the backs of
my eyes growing warmer, like they were burning up.

This whole town was already infected. We had no way of knowing
who was friend and who was foe.
…So the solution was clear. Let's just get *everybody* over here.
With that many *eyes* gathered together on one focal point…any
would-be villains would have to be a lot more careful about what
they tried.

The noise was growing into a rabble. I knew that thousands, tens
of thousands, even, were advancing upon the school. It was the first

time I ever used my "captivating eyes," the skill I hated so much this entire time, with all my strength.

The next thing I knew, the whole area was shining a beautiful gold. The moon, once hidden in the clouds, was now massive in the sky, shining with everything it had. Pretty fancy lighting for my final stage show. I sure couldn't hold back now.

I was ready to captivate this town, this nation, this world. I wouldn't allow them to so much as blink. I took another breath and shouted high into the sky:

"Momo Kisaragi, sixteen years old! —And I'm a pop idol!"

BLANKMIND WORDS 4

"…All right."

It was two in the afternoon on a sunny day in August, insects chirping in the trees. After sizing myself up in the full-length mirror and wrangling with a comb for half an hour, I finally managed to tame my bed hair down to submission.

"Wow…I'm really a girl."

I patted myself on the back. I had truly outdone myself: There was a frilly blouse, a dark-blue skirt—and a pair of shoes that had a cute blue ribbon on each toe. The Tsubomi Kido reflected in the mirror now was no longer the indolent sloth of old…or so I told myself.

Ever since Rin invited me on a shopping trip to town three days ago, I had been pawing through the hand-me-downs she lent me, obsessing over every potential choice. If I was just venturing out by myself, that would be one thing—but I was going to have my *sister* next to me the whole time. If I dressed in just any old thing, I couldn't even imagine how abashed I'd feel.

However, it certainly wasn't like I went out all that often. I had only the slimmest of knowledge about fashion, but I couldn't just go up to some servant and say, "Do me up so I look pretty and stuff, please." Thus, I had spent the past three days deliberating over the very core, the entire civilization, behind clothing. What seemed straightforward at first turned out to be an endlessly complex, meandering path, and it finally led me to this outfit.

I turned to my right side, then my left, twirling my skirt in the air. Even beyond the frontal view, I thought, *All right, I've made something of this…I guess. Like this, at least, pedestrians passing us by won't think, "Who's that stray mutt lurking at the feet of that ravishing young woman?"*

Stealing a glance at the old-fashioned clock on the wall, I realized it was almost time to go.

"…Well, here we are."

The moment I no longer had to worry about my outfit, I suddenly found my mind starting to race about other things. I had never gone shopping with someone before. What could I even discuss with her? *Just act natural, like you always do*, I said to myself. *But this girl staring at me in the mirror? That's not natural. It's not me. It's some kind of idealized Tsubomi from another world.*

I didn't know what my sister really intended when she invited me, but if I was leaving the house, I at least wanted her to have fun with me. But was I going to make it through today? Without making any clueless mistakes? Act properly, the way I was supposed to...?

There was a familiar knock on the door. I turned toward it. It was a bit early still, but I knew who it was as the door creaked open.

Rin smiled as she saw what I had done with myself.

"Wow. You look really cute in that, don't you?"

"Huh?! Uh—Th...thank you very much."

I thought she was deeply mistaken, but more than anything, I absolutely wasn't expecting any kind of compliment. I lowered my head down, feeling my cheeks catch fire. But my sister let out a little air, accompanied by a "hmph" that indicated something wasn't to her liking.

"Uh...hmmm..."

I struggled for words as she crossed her arms (now, *this* was back to normal for her) and stared at me. "Tsubomi," she said, "'thank you very much' isn't right, is it?"

This was a head scratcher. I thought I had expressed enough thanks for the praise. What didn't she like about it?

"...Ah!"

Then I realized why that wasn't good enough, and what my sister was expecting instead. I was filled with a creeping feeling of shame. It was hard to get used to some of her demands—but I made a promise, and I couldn't pretend I didn't...Well, here we go.

"Th-thanks! For...For the compliment!"

This was so embarrassing. If I looked in the mirror right now, the flames would probably be visibly roaring off my face.

"Hmm-hmm-hmm!" tittered my satisfied sister. I felt there was something a little melancholy to it, but maybe it was just my imagination.

Then, (once again) just like always, she patted me on the head.

"Well, great. Maybe you aren't quite used to it yet, but a promise is a promise. Try to see this through, all right?"

Despite all the talk of "seeing this through," this promise we enacted with each other really didn't involve a ton of heavy lifting on my part.

Last month, on that evening I ruined my sister's blouse with all my sobbing, my sister offered me a set of rules to follow. First, if either of us was feeling down about something, we would try not to hold it in—and tell the other person. That wasn't a promise, I supposed, as much as a suggestion for my sake. She talked about how I seemed to be the kind of person who bottled it all in if left to my own devices. I never noticed that part of me before. But since she was saying it, I reasoned, it had to be true.

She told me it wasn't a pain having me around at all, but looking back, I suppose that promise was based a lot on what happened out there by the gate that night.

Our second agreement was to not get worked up too much about our father. Listening to Rin, it sounded like the weird way he held himself was something that had bothered her for years. She had tried to reach out to him several times, but it was like grasping at air.

Maybe our father was a little strange, but if you thought about it, that was all he was. Not strange in an abusive way. He never forced us to do anything.

"I know he'll turn you off sometimes," Rin told me, "but I want you to just grin and bear it, all right?" I had no reason to shake my head at that.

Our third promise was the toughest one to carry out, but generally, it boiled down to: "We're sisters, so stop acting so formal around me!"

I was in total agreement about this. I didn't like it much myself, especially given how we were technically in the same family. I would have done away with it long ago if it weren't for the servants pushing it on me. "Proper etiquette reigns even among close circles," as they put it.

So I readily agreed to all three of those promises, but somehow, that third one was the toughest nut to crack. Once you fell into the habit of acting overly polite toward someone, it was nearly impossible to stop. I knew I shouldn't have tried keeping it up for so long. I doubted we would, but if we ever had a little brother or something to deal with, I'd make sure both of us ordered him to knock it off with the formalities. It'd be for his own sake.

"Well, if you're set to go, how about it? A pity it's so hot outside," Rin said, clearly distressed at the news. She must have not liked the heat at all, either.

"I'm all set, so that's fine by me, thank..."

She scowled at me.

"Uh, I'm ready! Let's do it!"

"Perfect. Shall we?" Rin relaxed her face again. Eesh. "I was thinking we could have some ice cream while we were out. There's this one place I've heard good things about, but do you like that kind of stuff?"

"Oh, I love it!"

I couldn't have asked for anything more. *Going shopping means that you get free ice cream, too?!*

"Well, in that case, get ready for as much of it as you can stand! Ooh, this is gonna be fun."

I was spellbound. *So she likes desserts, huh?* I thought as I took my purse off the back of my chair and joined her out the door. Then, without any particular thought behind it at all, I peeked at my room.

Nobody called me back in. I hadn't forgotten anything important. All I heard were the cicadas through the window I had left open for ventilation.

   ...Oh, but if I had but listened a little closer, I might have heard it. The sound of the long, lilting violin among the insect cries.

CHILDREN RECORD SIDE -NO. 3-

As I ran down the stairs, my eyes were greeted by a brand-new metallic wall painted white. We were at the floor we were seeking, and we had momentum. Once we made it through this hallway, we would be standing right in front of the room where the "clearing" was.

Shintaro, breathing hard, kept looking behind him. I could see he had an earbud in one ear.

"Geez, Momo…I told you to go all out, but I didn't mean *this* all out."

Just like he'd promised, the full, unhinged power of her "captivating eyes" was beyond belief. Even this far away from her, it took nearly all my mental concentration to force myself to think about anything besides the look, the feel, the concept of Momo Kisaragi. I couldn't believe she had the fortitude to keep it all under wraps until now. If this kept up, this whole event might just go down in history.

"I'd have to guess there's a crapload of people on the ground above us right now," I said. "I can't believe how much of a hit Kisaragi is."

"Yeah," Shintaro replied, taking another look back. "With enough people, the enemy won't be able to call for reinforcements at will. Assuming *he* can get Momo outta there like we planned, that should take care of things up there. But…*ugh*, I told her not to do anything dangerous, and now look…!"

Kisaragi's mission in this operation was to divert our foe and prevent them from calling for backup. I knew Shintaro said it, too: "Take absolute care, Momo, that you don't hurt yourself along the way." I guess Momo had gotten a little…okay, a lot carried away.

"Hey, she's doing her best for us, you know? I mean…we're all risking our lives here."

"Yeah, but there are certain limits, man," Shintaro whined as he turned his head back forward.

*   *   *

The twisty, undulating corridors forked with regularity, proceeding inward like a labyrinth deliberately built to stymie us. I had been here several times before, but it was the first time I could manage the traversal without any hesitation. It really all came down to Hibiya and his map, and that we made it this far in such a short time.

That "focusing eyes" skill is nuts. Totally nuts. We practiced it just a little bit last night, and Hibiya had it down. All he had to do was look at (or picture in his mind, really) his target, and he could recall several kinds of things about the target, just like that, right down to the last detail.

It was psychometry taken to absurd extremes. I showed him a photo of Dad just to test it out, and *bam*—he had a grip of this building's entire floor plan. Every nook and cranny.

We were hoping for some kind of basic map, but what he gave us was more like a road atlas. It shocked me. "I always liked mapping intricate structures and stuff" is how he explained it, but this might be some genius-level talent we had here.

As I marveled at Hibiya's mental prowess, Shintaro's phone rang. We stopped, eyes opened wide. This was the third phone call of the night, but that didn't make the mood among us any less frazzled than the previous two.

Shintaro picked up the phone, then pointed at the T intersection right in front of us.

"It—it's coming from the right! …You got it, Konoha?!"

His short white hair fluttered past for a single moment.

"…Okay!"

Konoha, perfectly silent up to now, followed Shintaro's command and leaped forward like a bullet. At the same moment, a man in white defensive gear appeared from the right-hand fork. He was armed with a handgun, and the moment he noticed us, he readied its sights on us.

"No you don't!"

Before he could even finish saying it, Konoha's right foot kicked the gun away. It clanked loudly against the ceiling. The man was surprised by it just long enough for Konoha's right knee to bury itself in his solar plexus.

"Whoooa," I couldn't help but say. It was like something out of an action film, as the man fell to the floor without so much as a shout. We checked to make sure he was out, then let out a sigh of relief.

"...Haah! How many of those bastards are there, anyway?!"

"I don't think there're any more nearby," Hibiya replied through the phone, "but be careful, all right?"

That was right...His "focusing eyes" were on us the whole time— exposing dangers in our path, offering advice. That was his job.

Konoha bowed politely at his fallen foe, then returned to us, a sorrowful look on his face.

"I...I really don't like hitting people, I guess."

It was so meek of him—too meek for someone who just pulled off that kung fu nonsense. He was averting his eyes, even.

Shintaro sighed and scratched his head. "Look, I know this is a pain in the ass for you, but it's kind of an emergency, you know? I think you're gonna have a break for a while, anyway."

Konoha visibly brightened at this, looking expectantly at Shintaro.

"Am...Am I being a help to you guys, Shintaro?"

"We're friends. It's a lot more than 'being a help.'" He smiled. "We're totally relying on you."

Nothing he said could've made Konoha happier.

Friends, huh? I think I'm starting to like the concept.

After catching our breath, we moved on, taking the next fork left and immediately finding the door we were after.

I felt a chill down my back. *It's here. Beyond this door. Our mortal enemy.*

Shintaro, sensing my nervousness, patted me on the shoulder.

"That's your dad in there, right? If you're his kid, it's time to give him a piece of your mind, okay?"

...Damn, Shintaro. You've got such a gift for words at times

like these. I hate to admit it, but I'm really gonna have to tell Kido about this.

Driven on, I approached the door. At Shintaro's signal, Konoha kicked it open.

The moment he did, I winced at the intense odor of formaldehyde.

Cables, in a variety of colors, lined the room. Experimental equipment was strewn around, and there was a countless number of monitors on the wall...

And there he was, deep inside the dimly lit laboratory, looking right at us from his seat. The glare from the monitors made it impossible to see his expression, but I could tell he was flashing a vulgar smile.

"Whoa, whoa, what're you doing smashing up someone's house in the middle of the night? You ever heard of proper discipline, you little brats?"

It was my dad's voice, but he had never talked like that. It was harsh, off-putting, like a snake licking its lips. There was no doubt now. *He* was now on the forefront.

"Heh," Shintaro grunted. "Sorry about that. We're all still in high school, y'know. If you don't like it, just try to lecture us about it."

He started walking into the lab, demonstrating not even the slightest iota of fear. There was no one else in the room, and none of us could even guess what kind of traps may have been set. It seemed incredibly brash, but you could see it on his face. That confidence. It hadn't dissipated at all. I wouldn't want to have anyone else on my side.

"Well...really, though? Just the three of you, advancing on me? That's really all you think of me, huh? And here I thought you were smarter than that."

His eyes were on me now. They were a deep crimson. That hateful, hateful color, one I'd never forgotten since that day. I tried to hold back my anger as I spoke:

"Yeah, well, we kinda got some promising new talent on our side, all right? And I don't think he's about to get taken down that easily... I think you know that."

The crimson eyes turned toward Konoha. Despite all his namby-pambiness of a moment ago, his mouth was now stretched out in a straight line, matching his gaze.

"I heard about you," he said, his monotone quietly echoing around the room. "Mr. Tateyama…No. The 'bad guy.' Trying to kill everyone…I can't let that happen."

Then the room was filled with exaggerated laughter. "Oh, come on—what's the big deal?" our nemesis said, rubbing his hair. "You've finally got the 'friends' you've wanted, too, huh?"

Shintaro stepped up to cut him off before he could continue with his breezy ravings. "We know about your scheme," he said. "About Azami…about the Kagerou Daze…and the way you want to kill them all so you can create a new Medusa."

It didn't faze Dad at all. Shintaro didn't let that stop him.

"I don't know why you're doing this, but it's over. Surrender right now and release everybody who's in your grasp. If you can't…" He pointed at Konoha. "We…Konoha's gonna mess you up."

Konoha snorted to accentuate the point.

Man. I feel pathetic right now. Shintaro should write all our dialogue for us.

There was a pause. Then my dad let out a deep, lazy sigh and finally got up off his chair.

Shintaro blinked. I didn't notice it in the dimness before, but our enemy had a gun in his right hand. Konoha steeled his body in response, ready to fight.

"Ugh," the man on the other side said. "I swear, why the hell do I have to put up with these little kids all the time…?"

He slowly raised his arm, pointing the gun at Shintaro as his crimson eyes drilled into him.

"N-no!"

The next moment, Konoha was between the two, both hands outstretched.

"D-don't be stupid, Konoha!" shouted a panicked Shintaro. "You're putting yourself in danger!"

"We—We need to stop this," Konoha said to the man he was facing. "It's gonna take more than a pistol to kill me...and I'm pretty sure I can beat you in an instant."

I knew Konoha's body was blessed with incredible physical and regenerative skills. According to what Kido told me, he had a huge hole blown in his stomach and was just fine afterward. That guy must've known that. It was obvious he had no chance.

"Ah, Konoha. Yeah, you've got a pretty sturdy body there. This one wouldn't stand a chance against you."

He sounded like he was ready to surrender. But his easy smile remained on his face, his finger still on the trigger.

"So...how 'bout this, then?"

He turned his gun. I thought it'd be on me, but it kept turning... until it was pointed straight at his own head.

"Ah...!" I couldn't help but shout out. "What're you doing?!"

"Hmm? What...? Isn't it plain as day? I'm gonna blow your father's brains out."

The sight made me recall the disgusting words I heard not long ago. There, on the roof that evening, he said, "I'm the one allowing both you and your family to stay alive."

Oh. So that's what he had meant. I thought he was talking about us—the kids. But he had meant he had our father's life in his hands.

"So, now what're you gonna do, you little brat? It's all your lives, or this guy's. Who's gonna win out?"

He was talking to Shintaro, standing stock-still behind the flustered Konoha. Asking him to decide who lives or dies...Nobody could ever do that. Especially someone with Shintaro's outlook on life.

"Hey, now," the gunman continued, twisted smile on his face, "don't keep me waiting. Hurry it up, or else I..."

"...I thought I told you. It's over."

The declaration from Shintaro made his smile crumble just a little.

"Uhh? What do you think you're saying?"

"Oh, you don't get it?" Shintaro said, his voice unwavering. "Well, lemme make it clear, then…"

Oh great. I was trying to hold it back, but now even I was grinning. *Shintaro's such a hoot. I love him.*

"Blindfold complete."

Suddenly, the room began to waver, a purple hood twirling in the air before us.

The white-haired girl who followed immediately after caught our mortal enemy in her sights. Without another word, he froze in place, returning the room to an uncanny quiet.

"…You mind not stealing my lines, Shintaro?" accused a nonplussed Kido.

"Oh, what's a little fun gonna hurt? I kinda needed to say something to round things out just now!"

Marie arched her brows at this. "It…I don't think it sounded that cool."

"Uh? But…nnnhhh…"

He brought both hands to his face and fell to his knees. *Aw, don't get so torn up over it, Shintaro. I thought it was kinda neat, myself. Not that I was gonna say it. Not around her.*

"…Right." Konoha poked at my dad's body a bit, then turned around. "Looks like he's immobile for a while."

Kido let out a sigh of relief. "…Man. That was one risky operation… but I guess it turned out all right. I thought we were dead once Marie ran out of breath on us…"

"Y-you guys all run too fast!" a puffy-cheeked Marie protested. "I tried calling for Kano, but he just left me behind…!"

"What do you want from us? We couldn't see you. We had no way of knowing. That's how the operation worked."

"Yeah," Shintaro interjected as he stood up and smiled. "But we all still had to be here, or else we couldn't have caught that guy off guard. But what's done is done, right? I was kinda scared when he brandished that gun, but..."

He was so calm and dignified just a moment ago, when he was talking down our nemesis. Now, there was no sign of it.

Ah, well. I kind of liked this Shintaro more, anyway.

The operation came as a major surprise when I first heard about it, but I had to admit, Shintaro solved everything for us. Along those lines, I just kinda sat there, stewing in my own juices...Never really did anything at all, in the end.

"When he took Dad hostage like that," I began, "I mean...Man, what a surprise. Like, wow, just like you said he would, Shintaro."

"Ah, it was just an estimated guess on my part," he replied modestly. "One way or another, I was planning to neutralize him with Marie's power, anyway."

"Yeah, but...I really owe you one. We could've just had Konoha restrain him or something, but you came up with a way to save Dad without hurting him...I dunno how to thank you."

"Ah, geez, quit it," Shintaro protested, blushing. "That's not like you at all."

Something about his act was familiar. I don't think Ayano ever noticed, but Shintaro always smiled at her in a different way from all of us. I never really dug that much. That's why I was always so cold to him when I started posing as her in school. Now I felt bad about being so mean to him in her form. *I'm hopeless.*

But despite all that, Shintaro let it slide. And now he was smiling at me...just like that.

Ahhh, I can't win against him. He's invincible.

"...So, what now?" Kido said, pointing at our frozen father. "We gotta do something before Marie's power wears off, don't we?"

"Oh, right. Konoha, did you bring it with you?"

"Uh, yeah. You mean this?"

Konoha took out a spool of metal wire.

"We're gonna tie him up with this and take him out of the hide-out," Shintaro explained. "Kido can use her ability to keep anyone from noticing us...and that oughta be it, really."

"Yeah," Kido added, eyes sparkling. "Whatever abilities he has, he won't be able to use them if he doesn't have a free body. After that, we can just put 'im through the wringer at our hideout until he coughs up some info on the Kagerou Daze..."

"Um, lemme remind you," I protested, "he *is* our father, so..."

"Oh, I know, I know. You ready, Konoha?"

At her command, Konoha began to wrap the wire around my father's body.

I never imagined in a million years we could actually stop him.

Or that any one of us actually had a future.

If things kept going this well, maybe we really could get my sister out of the Kagerou Daze. Maybe even our mother.

I'd never thought about that. Not even once.

What would I even say if I ran into them again? There was so much to talk about, I wouldn't know where to begin. But I knew they'd be smiling for me. Smiling, laughing, talking about all kinds of stuff...

...Like an idiot, I was imagining that impossible future right up to the moment that Konoha fell before my eyes.

When I woke up, I was lying down inside a dimly lit room. The cicadas that had driven me mad over the last few days were only barely audible. The space was filled with a cold, moldy sort of air, nothing like what you would normally feel in midsummer. It was interspersed with something…weird. Like nothing I'd ever smelled before.

Candlelight seemed to flicker off the rough-hewn stone walls around me. Wherever it was, it wasn't positioned well enough to illuminate the room, instead casting an endless multitude of constantly shifting shadows.

I looked around, eyes still not used to the dimness, until I had a vague idea of the room's outlines. Across from me in this stone room was a lone metallic door with a rectangular slit high enough for a grown adult to see through. Vertical iron bars lined it. On the right side, against the wall, there was a wooden bookshelf that rose to the ceiling; it was lined with several books and small flasks. Next to it was a Western-style suit of medieval armor with its right arm missing. It stood there motionless, carrying a lance in its remaining arm.

On the left-hand wall, there nothing to match the bookshelf—just a lone bag, similar to a burlap sack, with black stains all over it.

The candle was located next to the door, which was why its light had no hope of reaching me. That was the main reason I failed to notice my sister's presence next to me until I picked up on her frail breathing.

"Ahh…!"

She was standing against the stone wall behind me…or, really, that was her only choice. Both of her hands had shackles, each a couple of inches long, connected to the ceiling with chains. It looked like something out of a fantasy dungeon or POW camp.

This bizarre atmosphere threw me for a moment. Was this real? I wasn't having a dream, was I? But the damp air, the smell that accompanied it, and my sister's raspy breathing made it all too clear that that wasn't the case.

It wasn't a dream. I stood up and ran toward Rin.

"I—I can't…What happened to us…?!"

My sister wasn't conscious enough to respond. She was hanging down from the shackles, her weight placed entirely upon them. Even if I wanted to remove them, they were chained to the ceiling—far too high to reach. I took another look around. Nothing I could use as a stepstool.

All I could really do was prop Rin up a little so her entire weight wasn't on her wrists. So I did. I wrapped my arms around her waist, as if hugging her.

Ahh, aghhh, what is this?!

I thought I went out shopping with Rin that day. We went down to the city stores, ate ice cream, maybe purchased some matching handkerchiefs, ate dinner in Rin's room, and…Shoot. I couldn't remember the rest.

So how did *this* happen? Someone must have kidnapped us and then locked us up in here. But who, and what for? And where was "here," anyway? This stone room, with chains and shackles and an iron door…

"N-no way…"

A guess that popped into my mind made my body shake. I remember what my sister told me before: "Some burglars tried to sneak in here, and he trapped them inside a basement room, right in this manor." I thought she had made up the whole thing, including the entire presence of a basement—but if she hadn't…?

This is crazy. I don't get any of this. And even if that is the case, why us? My arms, still supporting Rin, began to quiver.

"Wh-why…Why this…?" There was no point in crying about it, but the tears welled up anyway. My daily life with Rin, all the inane conversations we had, felt so far out of reach. What was going to happen now? We were already locked in a space beyond all reality. I couldn't imagine anything worse.

Just when I thought I was going to collapse on the floor, a familiar delicate voice reached my ears.

"…Tsu-Tsubomi? You aren't hurt?"

The voice from my awakened sister was slow, listless, but still clear. I shook my head in response, forgetting how dark it was. It must have been a strong enough reaction to convince her I was fine.

"Good," she replied with a weak smile. We were still in grave danger, but just seeing Rin smile helped reduce the terror that reigned inside me.

I tried to tell her what I experienced. "I, um, when I woke up, I was here, and…and I don't remember…"

"No. Me neither. I don't remember anything after dinner. Maybe someone drugged us…I don't know what we're gonna do about this."

She jangled her chains at me. They were nothing she could remove by herself. I was the only one capable of doing anything about this situation. But what?

"Could you go check out the door? Maybe they forgot to lock it after all this. I doubt it, but…"

I examined the old metal door. There wasn't so much as a knob on it. Like she surmised, it was locked from the other side.

"I—I can't open it."

"Oh. It'd be nice if there was some other entrance…but what now?"

Rin looked around the room. Even during a disaster like this—this crazy room, those shackles—she showed zero sign of panic. She had to be scared out of her wits, deep inside. I knew she had to be. *She must be hiding it to keep me from getting anxious*, I thought as her eyes went from the door to the bookshelf, then the suit of armor.

That sight made her eyes open wide. "Wh-what's that doing here?"

I turned toward Rin, surprised at this sudden outburst. "You… know it?" I asked. My sister replied with a rueful grimace—she did, and she didn't want to say it. With a sigh and a deep breath, she began to speak.

"You see how there's no right arm on it? Back when I was a kid, I lost it while I was playing with it. That suit of armor wasn't anywhere near here back then."

"So this, this really is…"

Rin nodded. "I think it's the basement under the manor I told you about. And if I had to guess who put us in here…"

She was interrupted by a sudden dry sound from the other side of the door. It sounded like footsteps, one after the other, growing in sound as they approached.

I ran to my sister again, flustered at the presence of this new visitor. If someone was coming, it'd be for one of two reasons. To help us, or…

The footsteps stopped. The candle's meager light bounced off the pair of cold eyes peering through the slit in the door.

"Ahh…!"

It took just a single glance. Our father was there. But nothing he projected indicated he was flying in to rescue us.

Rin looked on grimly, glaring at the slit.

"I figured it'd be you, since you had the key, if anyone. What…are you doing with us? Whether we're family or not, this isn't any kind of joke I'm willing to tolerate."

"…Rin, have I ever joked with you before?"

I could feel my hair stand on end. It was the indifferent, emotionless delivery he had always used. My father didn't even try to deny it. He was the one who spirited us away in here.

My sister, as much as she could, stood her ground, her voice sharpening itself.

"That doesn't matter. Please, take us out of here. If you can do that right now, we won't tell anyone about it, so—"

There was a loud *ka-chank* from the door before she could finish. That must have unlocked the door, because then, with a shrill creak, it opened.

Our father stood there with the same inscrutable expression, the same white shirt and suit pants he always wore. Not a thing different about either. That's what made the *differences* seem all the starker.

In one hand, he held a gigantic cooking knife. The blade, just barely illuminated by the candle, was caked with something dark, a not-yet-congealed liquid dripping from the tip. There were spots running from the cuffs of his white shirt up to the front, like something was spattered on it.

I didn't even need to think about it. It was blood.

"Ah—aaahhh!"

It was so beyond reality that I screamed and clung to my sister. She tensed up her body in response—it was finally enough to unnerve her.

This elicited no reaction from our father as he stepped inside.

...*He's gonna kill us.* It was like no fear I had experienced before. My body refused to cooperate. It felt like it was going to blow itself apart, shivering violently like it was being lowered into a pot of boiling water.

My sister could do nothing to stop him. So she shouted at him instead.

"Wh-what do you think you're doing?! ...What's wrong with you?!"

Our father stopped. "What's wrong with me? Hmm. The servants upstairs said the same thing, come to think of it."

"What...?! So...so that blood..."

"Oh, you know—they all got into a little tizzy...Nothing for you to worry about, though."

I could feel my sister stirring in my arms. That much blood on him...He must've killed at least one person already.

"I'm a little short on time," he continued in his cold monotone. "If you have anything else you want to ask, I'd like you to be quick with it, please."

I found myself unable to process this situation anymore. I'm sure

Rin was the same way. Throwing us into this dungeon and killing people...No matter what the reason, it was the work of a madman. And yet my father wasn't raving or screaming at us. He was betraying no emotion whatsoever. No sense of normalcy or common sense could've prepared us for this. Instead, I just stayed there, shaking in terror.

But my sister refused to budge. I guessed she was trying to buy us time. Conversation was the only weapon either of us had left.

"Wh-what are you going to do with Mother? She already has enough mental issues to deal with..."

"...Oh, her? I'm not going to do anything. She's right there, isn't she?"

Our father's eyes swiveled down to the floor. Down to the burlap sack I'd noticed earlier.

"She's been in there...oh, right since the day you arrived, Tsubomi. I thought I mentioned that."

"Ahh...!"

My sister finally let a scream escape her lips. Her faint shivering resonated across my arms, and from there to my body. Then, she emitted a sound that no words could describe, sending it echoing across the room.

...I wanted to shut off my ears to it all. She's been in here since the day I showed up...? Now it was clear what gave this room its unique smell. I immediately grew nauseated.

A servant told me "the lady of the house's health has turned for the worse," but never anything like this. Our father must've lied about that to keep them from noticing the murder. That was exactly the type of person he was. Nobody would've dared question it. Then he could use his wife's ailing condition as a shield, creating a routine where he was the only one taking care of her. For months on end...

And here we thought our father had lost his sanity only today.

...This man isn't human. He's a monster in human skin.

*   *   *

I grabbed tightly at my sister's clothes. Unless something happened, we were absolutely going to be next. We had to get out of there. But Rin was shackled to the ceiling, and we probably needed a key for that. A key that, no doubt, our father had.

Rin began to openly weep. I couldn't imagine what she was feeling—her mother dead, her father turning a blade on her.

"...Is that all you have to ask?" he impatiently prodded. My sister looked down at the floor, no longer reacting to him, none of the refined elegance left in her eyes as the tears flowed from them.

Our father, apparently taking that as a yes, walked up to us. I could tell he was readying his grip on the knife in his hand.

What should I do? What could I do? I could never overpower him. So what, then...?

"...What, Tsubomi?"

I stood up to my father. My body took action before I could think of anything.

It wasn't that I was no longer terrified of him. I just couldn't forgive the man who, in this indescribably desperate situation, made my sister break down before my very eyes. I stood as tall as I could, breathing in the acrid air.

"...You said you'd answer anything we asked you?"

"Yeah..." He looked at me. "Do you have something?"

...Don't fall back. Speak to him, Tsubomi.

"Well, why are you doing this? Killing your wife, then the servants... Tell me why."

My father exhibited no reaction to my piercing stare. Which was good. If the question had angered him, that would be it right there. But I couldn't fold now. I had to buy some time, at least. And somehow, in some way, get out of this pit...!

Several seconds passed. My father sighed.

"...All right. I said I'd answer, so I'll tell you. About your mother."

"...What?"

I was thrown by the unexpected change of subject. I was asking him what drove him to commit this horrendous act, not wax nostalgic about the past. Or did my mother have something to do with this?

My father narrowed his eyes. "I...I wanted to live free. I had no interest whatsoever in the future my father had prepared. But I still went to the school he picked for me, took up the post he made, married this girl I had never met before at his bidding...It was like a living hell. It was my life, and I wasn't allowed to decide on a single part of it for myself. Then we had Rin, and then my father died...and I met your mother right around then."

His eyes right then, I thought, were filled with a passion I had never seen from him before.

"I had some clients entertaining me at this cheapo dinner theater, and she was singing there. It was this dinky little stage; maybe a handful of people in the audience, but she was acting like it was so much fun...I thought it was so stupid. This mature woman, screwing around in this dingy corner of the world. What was she thinking? ...But."

The words stopped. My father sighed again, staring at a point far away.

"I thought she was beautiful. Wild, innocent, totally uninhibited...That completely unencumbered soul she had. For the first time in my life, I felt true love."

I gasped.

No. This wasn't what I asked. Not this...

"It was like a dream after that. I set up my job so I had more chances to come back. She was a good listener—she didn't just sit there and praise everything I did; she taught me everything I lacked in my own life. When she had some time off, she even tried teaching me how to play music. Nothing very good, but still—I completely fell for her. I practiced hard, too. An older guy like me, trying to take up an instrument…I guess you heard me, didn't you? Pretty good, huh?"

"That was you…playing the violin?"

Now it all made sense. No wonder Rin had no idea. Our father never told us about this relationship. He only ever played in front of my mom.

"But that didn't last too long. Once she realized I already had a family, she disappeared from my life. She quit singing at the dinner theater; she changed addresses…It was hard. But I put up with it. As long as I was still alive, I figured it was fine. So I kept on practicing because I figured I could surprise her with that if we ever met again…I really thought that would happen someday. Until I heard she died."

My father grimaced a little. His face had never moved an atom before. It made him look extraordinarily pained.

I didn't care at all about my father or how he felt. But somehow, it pained me how much I understood his feelings. I knew more than anyone else how it felt to lose my mom.

"…I pretty much went to her funeral that day on a whim. She was dead, and it's not like I had any parting words for her. It was just…I was shocked. I never imagined you would be there."

He paused to size up my face. His was no longer cold and restrained. It was muddied, unclear, his eyes darting to and fro across my body.

"Tsubomi…You're my last hope. The family I had was like a pair of handcuffs, but you're different. I never want to let go of you again… And starting today, I'll be free of everything except for you. We can live together. I can give you anything you want. No matter what it takes…"

My father placed his left hand on my shoulder. I looked up at his face, and what I saw amazed me. He wasn't looking at me at all. I didn't see one bit of my reflection. All I saw was his firm belief that I was *my mother's* daughter.

His boundless, hollow eyes confirmed my belief.

*   *   *

This man…was beyond saving.

At that moment, my sister's leg came across me and kicked our father on the side. The cooking knife in his hand clanked heavily to the floor.

"Nnh…!"

He doubled over. Before I could think, I extended my hand. It was now or never. It was in my sights. I had to get that knife…!

Just as my hand was about to clasp the handle, a sharp pain crossed my right cheek. The sight of the knife, just an inch or two from my hand, defocused and flew away. The next moment, my body was thrown to the feet of the suit of armor.

"Tsubomi!"

The armor collapsed, falling to the floor with a powerful clatter. I could just barely hear my sister shouting over the noise. My father's right arm was in my bleary vision; he must have slapped it away in the nick of time. Slowly, he picked it up and started walking toward my sister, gazing down at her, his expression not recognizable as human.

The worst outcome imaginable crossed my mind. My vocal cords vibrated like they would catch on fire.

"Stooooop!!"

My father glanced back at me, then returned his hateful stare to Rin. "You…You played your stupid sister games with Tsubomi to trick her! I should have known…When I told you to get her back here for me…You must've fed her a pack of lies right then, didn't you?"

When she…"A pack of lies"? What is he talking about?

"I simply told her what I needed to," Rin said, her voice thundering across the chamber. "As her sister. This girl isn't some kind of doll for you to play with. You can't shut her in here. You won't even let her set foot outside the house! It's crazy!"

Something snapped in my father when he heard this. He slowly raised the knife, the candle's glint reflecting in it, and blinked menacingly.

Memories of the short time I spent with Rin ran through my head.

The first time we met, I honestly thought she was scary. She chided me for every mistake I made, and nothing ever escaped her notice. My inability to express my feelings exasperated me sometimes.

...So what did I find happy about the time I spent with her? The way she praised me when I managed to get my feelings across? Or when she patted me on the head and called me "cute"?

That all played a part, but I didn't think it was the number-one reason. Listening to my father, I knew what that was now. It didn't matter how Rin was related to me...

—She accepted me as her one and only sister.

I could feel something in my hand. I knew full well that the other end had plunged into flesh. My father looked at me, face clearly racked with shock. None of the coldness from before. It looked human. An actual human emotion.

Just as his eyes rolled up and he fell, the metal handle flew away from my hands. With another clank, my father hit the floor, the lance sticking out of him. In another few moments, he stopped moving. The helm on the armor, now at rest on the floor, quietly enjoyed the view of its weapon's final landing point.

I turned around. My sister was looking at me, biting her lip. Was she surprised or sad? I didn't have the words to describe her expression. I couldn't think of anything, but my shaking lips still parted.

"I...I think we're alone now, ma'am."

This elicited another hard-to-describe facial reaction. I wasn't sure how to put it, but it was similar to the face she made whenever she patted my head.

"I told you to stop being so formal with me…Tsubomi."

Her words brought tears to my eyes…

…only to have them shaken by the sound of a large, door-rattling explosion. It came so suddenly that I fell right to the floor.

Then there was another. A whole series of bursts, sending dust falling from the ceiling with every earth-rumbling blast.

"Wh-what's that…?!"

Something terrible was happening above us. I flew to my feet and more or less threw the door open with a shoulder. There was a staircase right beyond, with something like a half-open window at the top. I assumed it led to somewhere on the manor's ground floor.

I had to find out what was going on up there. The moment I placed a foot on the first step, there was another tremendous shaking and explosion.

"Ngh…!"

I instinctively stopped and closed my eyes. I thought it was the kickoff to another series of blasts, but we were greeted with only silence.

I waited for a few moments before slowly, gingerly opening my eyes. I couldn't believe what I saw.

"This…This couldn't…"

The window at the top had been shattered, crushed by a half-burned wooden beam. Embers were shooting down on me from the hole.

I stood there, dumbfounded, until my sister's voice rang out.

"Tsubomi! What's going on out there? What can you see?"

I turned around to look at Rin. She must have already known the answer. "I can't believe it," she added sourly.

What did my father say? "…Starting today, I'll be free of everything except for you." That, and "I'm a little short on time." If "everything" meant this entire manor, too…

"...Father must've set the house on fire. I suppose he planned to take you out of here and escape before the flames got us all."

As always, my sister was way ahead of me. I had no idea how far our father's plan went, but there was no doubt about his deranged state at the end of his life. Did he really want to bring me out of here? Or maybe, from the very start...

I shook my head, brushing my thoughts away. Right then, I had to find a way to unshackle my sister and get out of there. Right. The shackles, the shackles...

My heart skipped a beat. I couldn't think of a single way to take them off. There was no way I could reach them—not without something to stand on. And we were in the middle of a fire. Even if I was willing to forage through the flames for something, there was a giant hunk of wood jutting into the window. There was just barely enough width left for maybe one person to wriggle through—but no space for anything that could serve as a platform.

And come to think of it, I still hadn't confirmed something that I reasoned was probably kind of important.

I rushed back into the room and fumbled through my father's pockets. Into one, into the next, and then...

"There's no key...!"

I suppose I should have expected that. He was planning to be "free of everything." Yet again, the depths of his madness battered me down. He never intended to free Rin in the first place. The key was probably somewhere upstairs, but I didn't like my chances of finding such a tiny key in an inferno.

So now what? What can I do, in the time I have left...?

...No. Don't give up. Think! Whether I've got the key or not, there's got to be some way left to rescue my sister. I know there is. There's got to be something. Hurry. Hurry up and think! Think, think, think...!

"...It's fine, Tsubomi."

I'm sure I must've looked shattered when I turned around at Rin's voice. There was something in me that was still struggling to keep myself together, even though I knew there was nothing I could do… and that face finally snapped it apart.

Once she saw it, my sister gave a weak smile. "Thanks for trying so hard for me," she said softly. "You've given me something nice to remember. Now get out of here. You can still save—"

"…No."

Rin's face saddened at the interruption. Maybe, with my smaller body, I could run a perfect route through the house and escape in time. I knew that. I knew it full well.

But my sister was making a mistake. I…I didn't want to escape *together* with her. All I wanted was for her to be safe.

"I…I mean, even if I ran on you, I'd never be able to live…"

The blood from my father was pooling at my feet. A pool that I had made. I'd killed my own father. I was tainted. Even if we escaped together, I'd never get to be near Rin again. And the concept of walking a dark, blood-stained path for the rest of my life seemed… unthinkable.

"No. It's not your fault. You protected me, didn't you? You can't say you'll be unable to…Ahh!"

Another explosion, this one far larger than the others, ripped through the house, stopping my sister cold. We were close to the time limit.

A time limit, huh…? Maybe calling it "game over" would be more appropriate.

I ran up to my sister and hugged her as hard as I could. No longer did I need any of the words I learned to express my feelings. All I did was bring my face as close to hers as I could.

The explosion that followed was enough to make the sturdy-looking stone walls around us visibly start to rattle and fall. My sister's words no longer reached me. A deafening creak dominated them, as the collapsing, fiery ceiling crushed and splintered the bookshelf. The heat blowing down from above toasted the air gathered below, making it hard to even breathe.

The scene through the upstairs portal looked like hell itself. The charred furniture began to drop down above the collapsed ceiling like an avalanche. I stared unblinkingly at the chandelier, shining as it reflected the bright orange around it.

...And then, right at the end, a large black mouth appeared before me, driving away the inferno surrounding us on all sides. That was about all I remembered from my otherwise-erased memories.

"Wh-why...?"

With that single short word, Konoha collapsed to the ground. Looking over there, I found that Dad's body, which Konoha had been trying to tie up, was also completely limp, like a puppet whose strings were cut.

It was so weird. Marie's power should have lasted much longer. What could have happened...?

"Get—get out of here...!"

The moment the voice shouted that, a thick black shadow jumped out of Konoha's body. It enveloped him, instantly swallowing him within itself.

Marie screamed.

I had seen that once before.

When we were at Marie's place the day before...When Konoha got injured. The shadow was there then, too. But Konoha was totally unhurt now. Why had it appeared again?

The air around us was disturbing. Konoha's body, now a mass of sheer blackness, seemed to twist and turn on the ground as it transformed.

"H-hey!" Shintaro shouted. "Konoha! Can you hear me?! Shit...! What the hell is happening?!"

He tried to get closer, but a twisted, sickening voice rang out:

"N-no...No. Get—get away...!!"

I shuddered. That couldn't possibly be Konoha's voice. But it didn't stop Shintaro.

"Hang on! I'm gonna help you out...!"

He extended a hand into the shadow...and it vanished, as if evaporating into thin air.

A lone man stood where the shadow had been. He had a sinister sneer and jet-black hair. The face was a dead ringer for Konoha's, but the atmosphere was like nothing our friend exuded.

When he spoke, it was in Konoha's voice:
"...Game over, you little brats."

The anti-Konoha opened his eyes. It was a look so ominous that I screamed:
"Shintaro!! Get out of there!!"
But I knew the moment I did that I was already too late.

With unbelievable speed, the man brought his hand up to Shintaro's neck, grabbing him at the throat...and tearing it off.
Shintaro's body bent back, crashing into the monitors behind him as he fell to the floor. The blood spurting out made dreadful sounds, forming large pools on the floor as he lay there, limply.

"Ah...ahh..."
I couldn't speak. All I could do was spout off a pathetic-sounding groan. The other two were loudly shouting something or other.
Damn it. I had to think of something. We have to escape from this guy, or else all of us are...

The shadow man picked up the handgun from the floor, gave it an appreciative look, and pointed it at me.
My body stopped listening to my orders. A pure white filled my mind.

And the last thing that reached my ears were the words I never, ever wanted to hear from his mouth:

"...See you later, boss."

BLANKMIND WORDS 6

I had heard all about how people got sent to hell if they did bad things in life. That was common knowledge. I didn't even remember where I first learned it.

But try as I might to picture what "hell" looked like, all I could conjure up were fictional images drawn by old Japanese artists.

Nobody had ever brought a camera there, after all. And these days, if you wanted a photo of pretty much any place in the entire world, you had your choice of spots. If you didn't, it likely meant the location wasn't even worth spending the few seconds required to point and shoot.

But it was weird to me. The idea that this place where "bad people" went to—a spot visited by millions over the years, no doubt—was depicted only in the form of classical art. Why was that?

The answer was simple: because it was a superstition. A place where only the dead could go—there was no way a living person could learn about it in detail.

Hell was just a fairy tale made up by someone to shame the bad guys into being good. Even as a kid, I could tell that much.

That's what I thought...but apparently, truth could be stranger than fiction.

In August, fire consumed my body, and I died.

I hadn't confirmed that beyond all doubt, but I was confident in saying it. I was surrounded by the rising flames, my throat was crying out in pain as the air burned through it, and my vision went black. If I didn't die then, that would be pretty darn incredible.

And since dying, I had come to realize a few things. First, that I was still capable of thought. That was a surprise, to be honest. I had pondered, now and then, what it was like to die. For the most part, I was satisfied with the idea that it was probably like sleeping—you just didn't feel anything anymore.

If I was still thinking, though, that meant I was still using my brain. You'd think the flames would've burned that to a crisp, along with the rest of my body. But if I was still conscious and thinking, did that mean there was actually such a thing as a soul or whatever? Maybe. I wasn't exactly sure.

And also this:

I didn't know if it was hell or not, but it turned out there really was a place called the afterlife. I think. There's no way to impartially prove that this place I was in was the afterlife, so it's still just a theory for now. It's just that I died, and now I was hanging around there, so it seemed sensible to think this was the place.

And that's just what I was doing. Sitting down there, right smack dab in the middle of the afterlife.

I say "middle" just for a frame of reference. In reality, it's completely dark on all sides, so I couldn't really say where I was. There's certainly no map or signposts to turn to. Of course, I couldn't imagine what was going to happen next, either.

It was pretty clear to me that this wasn't "heaven," at least. No idyllic flower gardens or cute little cherubs. In terms of first impressions, this definitely seemed like "hell." Plus...I think I kinda knew why I was there. I killed my father with my own two hands. It wouldn't surprise me at all to wind up in hell.

So I couldn't save Rin in the end. Who could say what she saw there, amid that burning mansion? I think I heard something from her, but my memory of those final moments was hazy—and I sure couldn't ask her now. Everything was too late.

Inside this darkness, my consciousness seemed unusually sharp. This meant, I assumed, that I wasn't disappearing anytime soon. Forcing me to sit here, in a place like this, forever...God could come up with some nasty tricks sometimes. "Hell" was completely deserving of the name. I probably would've cried, if I could, but I couldn't shed any tears now. I just sat there, while time swam by in the darkness.

Ahh, this must be what loneliness is. I thought that life when I started living at the mansion was already lonely enough, but compared to that, I was positively blessed in there. I was so lonely now, I couldn't help but speak up.

"…Is anybody there?"

There couldn't be. I knew that. I was just using the words to hurt myself even more. There was no response, no one materializing to pat me on the shoulder.

But what about *that*: a faint light, far out in the distance, that didn't exist before I spoke? My heart leaped, not expecting this rapid turn of events. The flickering light was small as it floated in the dark, but nothing could've been more precious to me.

I stood up and made a beeline for it. I knew it might be another punishment—a phantom light that I could never reach, no matter how long I walked. But my feet didn't stop. I just wanted to cling on to something.

After a little while, the light began to grow, gradually revealing its true nature. I could see its shape, its size—and once I was almost there, I stopped. I ran nearly the whole way, but I wasn't panting at all. *I must really be dead, then.* In the afterlife. It had to be. I was sure I was right…

"…But what's a house doing in here?"

In front of me stood a neat little Western-style house, one totally out of place in this world of black. I took another look around, but there was nothing else nearby—nor any other physical objects, actually. Apropos of nothing, there was a single fairy-tale house plopped right into the dark.

…This would make a nice out-of-the-way restaurant.

No. That's just silly talk. Unless there were more dead people roaming around, they'd have a terrible time building a customer base. Oh, but wait—that's not impossible, is it? There's a lot I've only learned after dying. Things that seemed like a given before didn't seem quite that way now.

Maybe hell isn't how I pictured it at all. Maybe there's a nice Grim Reaper in there who'll treat me to some warm soup. I didn't have anywhere else to go, anyway. I had nothing to lose.

So I strode up to the wooden front door and gave it a knock.

…No response.

I thought about opening it up, but even in the afterlife, I still felt compelled to mind my manners. I was just about to dare a second knock when the door soundlessly opened.

I was greeted by a young woman dressed in clothing I would describe as a tad eccentric. "…What kind of a joke is this?" she said.

She was short, and her frizzy black hair was tied back with a red piece of fabric. It was hard to tell due to the inky blackness outside, but her hair had a lot of kinkiness to it—in fact, it was practically twisting and squirming underneath the tie.

My presence must've surprised her. She sized me up, eyes opening wider and wider. Perhaps she didn't see many visitors. So much for the restaurant idea.

"Um…where am I?"

That was all I could get out before she slammed the door in my face.

I was expecting that to some extent, but being so overtly rejected like that was enough to hurt anyone's feelings a little. She could've listened to at least a word or two.

After standing there frozen for a few moments, the door opened again. Not all the way—just a few inches, so she could peer through the crack at me. I could tell she was suspicious.

"…What are you?"

What am I? That's an odd way to put it. I decided to do the polite thing and answer.

"I'm…Tsubomi. What about you?"

I scared her once again. Her eyes burst open again, as if to say "Whoa, she actually answered me." Being asked her name must've disturbed her for some reason. "Wh-why," she retorted, "do I have to tell you?"

This struck me as a mean way to answer a question. I pouted a bit, deciding to take more of a curt tone.

"You're the one who asked me first. Why can't you tell me yours, too?"

The eyes peering at me bobbed upward, perhaps not expecting this full-court press.

"A...Azami."

"Azami...? Azami what?"

"Huh? Nothing. Just Azami."

Glad to see we were on a first-name basis this early on. Well, fine by me. No reason to be polite with her, either, then. Looking at her, though, she didn't seem like a violent person. *Maybe she'll tell me where I am once we get to talking.*

"So do you live here? I wanted to ask you a few questions."

"And I want to ask you a few, woman," Azami feebly replied, refusing to open the door any farther. "Why are you here? What do you want?"

This behavior was starting to make me feel like the wolf in a fairy tale. This was getting nowhere. But I still felt an obligation to answer her queries. If I got any further on her wrong side and she locked the door, I'd be completely lost.

"Umm...I don't really want anything. I just woke up, and I was in here. I don't have any idea how I got here...I think it's because I'm dead, though."

Was that a decent enough response? Hopefully, because that was all I could give her. Besides, this girl must have known a ton more than I did. Still, I began to feel like we were not seeing eye to eye.

Nonetheless, something in what I said made this Azami arch her eyebrows high. "Dead...? Did...Did you get swallowed up when you died?!"

"Swallowed up? ...Oh."

Come to think of it, I remembered seeing this gigantic mouth just before the big moment. I don't know if I fell in or not, but that must have been what she meant.

"Yeah, uh...I think I saw something like that."

"You did?! Tell me more! Every detail!"

Now I had her attention. Not that it drove her to open the door.

"All right," I said, getting a little irritated. "Could you let me in first? I'll tell you everything then."

Azami, fidgeting to and fro up to now, stopped. She didn't seem to be a fan of the suggestion. "You aren't thinking about doing something funny, are you?" she asked after a few moments.

What's she mean, something funny? Did she think I was going to swallow her whole or push her into the oven?

"I'm not, I'm not. I mean, what is it about me that's frightening you?"

That got the door open. I must have convinced her. "…Get in," she said before turning on her heels and walking away.

I followed her in, only to find that the inside of the house was even more of a fantasy realm than the outside. Bookshelves lined the walls from floor to ceiling, packed to the gills with what looked like a bunch of very old books. It was decorated kind of like the mansion I used to call home, although there wasn't any stomach-churning gaudiness.

That only added to the cute coziness of it. In terms of whether I liked it or not, I can only say that I preferred it to my old home by leaps and bounds.

As I took in the room, Azami eyed me even more suspiciously than before.

"You…You won't find anything valuable in here."

She thought I was going to ransack the place for jewelry or something? Talk about paranoia.

"I'm not thinking about taking anything, I promise…"

"Hmph," Azami snorted, pointing at a small chair by the window. "Sit down."

I did as told. There was another, equally small table nearby, just tall enough to rest your elbows on. It was the perfect little furniture set for having tea and taking in some light reading.

Azami settled down on the seat opposite me, then carefully studied my face. Judging by her body language, I figured I was the first guest she had seen in ages. She immediately kicked off our meeting with "What kind of joke is this?" so for all I knew, I could be the first visitor ever.

But the more I thought about this house—as neatly furnished as it was—the more it seemed eerie. There was no town, nor anything else, near her, but she had books, a table, some chairs…Where did she get them from?

There was a ton I wanted to ask, and not just about this world. Azami didn't seem willing to talk unless I started, so I spoke up.

"So…where am I, anyway? I guess you're living by yourself, but do you know anything?"

Azami's face hardened at the question. "Do I know anything? Of course I do. I created this."

…Did I hear that right?

"Um…You created this house?"

This only served to further irk Azami.

"My husband built this place. I'm saying that I created this world."

I could tell we were having trouble understanding each other. Azami created this world of darkness? How could this petite woman do something as divine as that? It was hard to believe. I stared at her for a moment.

"Don't believe me, do you?" she said in reply, clearly annoyed. Then she averted her eyes.

I couldn't afford to offend this woman any further. But I couldn't just swallow it, either. I decided to go for the truth:

"It's not that…I just mean, it's not like some regular person can create a world…"

"Some *regular* person…?" Something about what I said made Azami hold her mouth open. She reacted to the most unexpected things. "Do you think I'm human, woman?"

"Huh? Well, uh, yeah, I thought you were a normal girl…"

Then I noticed it. The twisting hair behind her red eyes. The scales ever so slightly running down her cheeks. I thought it was a bit odd at first, but nothing about that seemed to be makeup. The more I looked at Azami, the more I was convinced of that.

"You…*aren't* human?" I said.

"You are such a weird creature," she brusquely muttered.

I really think you're being the weird one here, but...

I mean, her calling herself nonhuman was, in and of itself, unbelievable.

It wasn't like her looks were totally inexplicable. Hollywood could do all kinds of tricks with makeup, turning actors into horrible monsters. That explanation seemed a lot more realistic to me. But once again, that assumed the existence of "reality" in the first place. I was dead. That I was carrying on a conversation right now was, in itself, unrealistic.

So if Azami wasn't a human being, that meant I didn't have any evidence to prove that she didn't create this world, either. I was approaching this from totally the wrong angle. Reality as I knew it had nothing to do with the realm I'd found myself in.

If I was going to keep up this chat with Azami, the first thing I had to do was take all my preconceptions about "reality" and toss them right out the window.

"...All right. I'm sorry. I kind of doubted you a little."

"Oh, it's fine," Azami replied, watching me like I was some rare, precious bauble.

There was a pause. I gave it another try. "So, about here...I originally thought that this was hell or...something."

"Hell? Oh, that silly superstition you humans created for yourselves? How could something like that ever exist?"

"Maybe not, but this sure seems a lot like it to me. Like, how did you even create this, Azami?"

There was nothing but black emptiness out the window. I doubt she took a giant paintbrush and daubed black over everything. Figuring out how to create huge new spaces was itself, after all, beyond the bounds of reality. I was starting to take an honest interest in this character before me.

"I'm not like you humans," she said distractedly, her face back to her usual glare. "I can do well near anything I fancy. With my abilities, crafting a world like this is child's play."

She gave me a prideful smile.

Child's play to create a world? That really *was* in the realm of gods. Maybe Azami was something like that, then? Something in me wanted to see it happen. I soldiered on.

"It's that easy? Could you just, like, make one right now?"

Azami's shoulders shook at the question. "Not…now, no."

"…So what *can* you do?"

"I…Not very much." She slumped her eyes downward, the confidence of ten seconds ago gone. I started to feel like she was just messing with me. "I left most of my abilities in my body when I came here. Right now, talking to you is about all I can muster."

Now she looked nearly ready to cry. *So is she this amazing goddess, or not?* I was having trouble following.

"Oh," I said.

This clearly offended Azami. "You don't believe me, do you? Well, fine. Once I regain my abilities, I'll make sure you're the one who gets to experience them first!"

No, um…You really don't have to, thanks. Though I suppose I didn't have much reason to doubt her. Feeding me a line didn't serve to help her at all, and it wasn't like my luck was about to get any worse, regardless. Going forward, I decided to just assume she was being truthful.

"But, I mean…abilities? What do you mean, you 'left your body'? Your body's right here, Azami."

Azami let out a sigh. "Maybe it looks that way, but it's not. I'm using a power that I call 'awakening eyes' that lets me move around by my consciousness alone."

"Awakening eyes"? Pretty fancy name. But that wasn't the full explanation I had hoped for. What did she mean by "my consciousness alone"? I arched an eyebrow at her.

"I suppose you would describe it as my 'soul,'" she added. "That's all that remains of me."

Ah. That makes more sense. But…wait a second. Does that mean…?

"So…so are you some kind of ghost…?"

"Like *you're* not," came the exasperated reply.

She had a point. It was annoying, how being dead didn't feel the part at all.

Azami looked out the window. "A long time ago," she said in a complaining voice, "I was tricked by this evil presence. I had my body taken from me, my family…Everything. I managed to escape alive, but without any of my abilities, I'm helpless."

This story was sounding more pitiful with every new development. *Does that mean she's been alone here the whole time?* Just being alone for a little while was enough to give me cabin fever. Her, on the other hand…

"…Well, can't you get your body back? Like, break into that evil guy's hideout, or…?"

Azami gave me a wistful grin. "Even if this spirit was back in my body, I still couldn't accomplish much. I've lost my 'combining eyes' skill—the one that grants me control over all the other skills."

"You lost it? Did you drop it somewhere?"

"No. It doesn't work that way. I gave it to my granddaughter…so she could live." Her voice took on a weary tone as her eyes narrowed. "She's in the outside world now. I hope she's doing all right. Not too lonely, I fear."

I could tell that tears were starting to form in Azami's crimson-red eyes. I knew full well how painful it was to be separated from your family. It must have hurt her just as badly, never getting to see her grand—

…Huh?

"A-Azami, you're a grandmother?!"

"Mm? What? What's so strange about that?"

Strange? At the very, *very* most, Azami looked to be around twenty. Not at all old enough for anyone to call her "Granny." All this talk about creating worlds and existing in spirit form was so astounding, it made me all the readier to believe it—but a grandmother? With those looks?

…Ugh. This isn't working. My imagination's going wild on me. It's making me lose my suspension of disbelief!

"I told you!" Azami suddenly erupted into laughter. "I'm not a human being! I don't age like you, and my external appearance never changes." She paused to wipe a tear from the outside edge of her eye. "I tell you, I never thought the day would come when I'd speak to another human being like him. You are so entertaining."

She probably didn't mean that ironically, but having someone laugh at me to the point of tears was a tad embarrassing. I could feel myself blushing. Time to change the subject.

"Uh, b-by the way! What did you want to ask me, Azami? You acted like my showing up was a huge surprise…"

Azami responded with a look of ignorance at first before the realization kicked on. "Ah yes! You said you were swallowed up at the moment of death before making your way here. Are you sure about that?"

"Um? Uh…I think so, probably." I only said it because I wanted her to open the door, but she was right, anyway. The searing flames, the giant open mouth…Everything else around me the instant death arrived was hazy by comparison, but for some reason, that image was etched into my mind.

"Were…Were you alone at the time? You weren't with anyone else, were you…?"

"Um…I was with my sister."

Azami visibly paled.

"Wh-what? Is that bad?"

"Right now, I can't issue any commands to the Kagerou Daze… This world we're in. I had my suspicions, but I never thought it'd actually happen…"

Kagerou…Daze? Is that the name Azami gave it? I didn't know what it meant…but I kinda liked the feel of it. But if she couldn't "issue any commands" to it, did that mean it was beyond her control?

She mentioned that most of her abilities were left with her body; maybe that has something to do with it. But how's it all connect with me being sucked into this world?

"What do you mean?" I asked.

"Back when I still had power over this world," Azami replied with

some reluctance, "my daughter and granddaughter were attacked by humans in the world outside the Kagerou Daze. They were both in a horrible state…I couldn't bear to see it, so I casually issued an order to my world: 'Bring in two people on the brink of death.' But when they arrived, they were already lifeless, so I had to give them replacement lives."

"Replacement lives…?" Something like the "souls" Azami mentioned earlier? I waited for Azami to continue, only to see her bring both palms out in front of her.

"I originally held sway over ten different powers. It turns out these could be used as a replacement for human lives, but apparently, different powers could be more, or less, compatible with certain people. And sadly, both my daughter and her daughter were compatible with just one power—the same one, my 'combining eyes.' The power I used to control the Kagerou Daze itself."

Her voice began to shake.

"I had no idea which one I should breathe 'life' back into. But my daughter stepped up and told me…She wanted me to give it to her own child. That she didn't need it. So…"

She could go on no further. She started sobbing.

…It was so incredibly cruel. If only one "life" could work for the two of them and it couldn't be split up, one would naturally have to decide which would be resurrected and which condemned to death. But her daughter gave up her lone chance for the sake of her own child—Azami's granddaughter. I could only assume she was gone forever.

"…Ever since then," Azami continued, still sniffling, "I haven't been able to handle any of my own abilities, much less the Kagerou Daze. I've still hung on to my 'opening eyes' skill, if barely, but there's no telling when it may disappear…"

Azami looked down at her palms, face tinged with anxiety. The abilities that take the place of lives, the true nature of this world…It was so far beyond the realms of reality, but her story all fit together, oddly enough. It didn't feel like she was lying. But something still didn't make sense.

"All right. I understand that…but, Azami, what does that have to do with me getting swallowed into this world?"

Azami looked terribly pained. "Don't you see?" she sobbed out. "I ordered the Kagerou Daze to 'bring in two people on the brink of death.' I never told it to stop!"

I had trouble digesting this for a moment.

Presumably, Azami lost the ability to give orders with that final one—which was "bring in two people on the brink of death." My mind began to construct a theory that I didn't like much.

"Wait…So you mean…"

Azami quietly nodded.

"The Kagerou Daze is sucking in 'two people on the brink of death' over and over again. Bringing them in here, into this world without time, leaving them to wander aimlessly without even being granted the gift of death. Just like it did to you."

Her blood-red eyes, laden with sadness, turned toward me. I felt like my heart was about to skip a beat. It would have, normally. That was how twisted and confused my head was. But my heart wasn't racing—or, for that matter, moving at all. It was long over for me.

I knew Azami wasn't lying. If she wanted to unnerve me, she could've told me all kinds of scarier tales…and if it was a lie, her eyes wouldn't have been that sad.

Kagerou Daze…A world without time.

If it's been set to take in people two at a time, that must mean my sister is somewhere in here as well. Sitting somewhere in the dark, just like I was before I encountered Azami…

If "dying" means not feeling anything anymore…then this really is hell in the end, isn't it? We're going to be locked in here forever, never dying, never disappearing. But it was odd how I didn't feel anything in the way of fear. Just a seemingly boundless sadness, one that filled all my heart.

*   *   *

"...Wh-why can you use *that*?!" Azami suddenly shouted at me. Her crimson eyes were wide open again, just like when we first met. I wasn't sure what she meant by "using" anything. I hadn't done anything in particular, apart from sit by the table, lost in thought.

"Huh? What do you mean by 'that'...?"

Azami got up off her chair, ignoring me. Then, without warning, she thrusted her arm toward my chest.

"Whoa!" I shouted in surprise, standing and turning around to dodge it. "What're you doing? Did I do something I shouldn't have...?"

My voice stopped at Azami's behavior. I was turned away from her, standing on the opposite edge of the window in front of the chair. She, meanwhile, was pawing at the air above the chair I had been sitting on before, like a cat playing with a toy. She kept intoning "Hey...Hey...!" as she did, like some kind of mantra.

...*Great. I broke Azami.* All the worry about her granddaughter must've pushed her over the brink. But I couldn't blame her; her story was compellingly sad, something that came across all too clearly as she relayed it. Just talking about her must have made something crack in her mind.

I felt terrible about it, enough so that I decided to give Azami, still shouting "Hey!" repeatedly, a reassuring pat.

"Aaaagh!!"

She leaped up on the spot and fell, taking the table with her. I reared back, put off by this even more bizarre behavior. I had no idea what was driving her to act like this. She rubbed her now-tender hip a bit, then glared at me so sharply I could almost hear the *zing* sound effect.

"Wh-why'd you have to surprise me like that? What are you thinking, you fool?!"

"Fool?" I shot back, resentful of this sudden barrage. "I was just worrying about you! Besides, why were you ignoring me just now?!"

"Nnngh...," she said, faltering at my verbal attack. I thought she was going to fire back; getting that reaction instead was something of a letdown. Considering her attitude, she was kind of a wimp, I supposed.

Azami, still on the floor, pointed up at me. "Y-you're the one who vanished into thin air," she said, more softly this time. "You can't expect me to hear you when you've disappeared like that."

"Disappeared? What are you even talking about?"

She limply curled back her finger, her face in total confusion. "You just used 'concealing' on me, didn't you? How do you expect me to see you then?"

...*This is a waste of time. What is this girl even saying? It was getting annoying*, I thought as Azami gasped once again.

"W-wait," she said. "Did you use that unconsciously...?"

"I told you," I shouted, "I have no idea what you're talking about! Start making sense for a change!"

Azami shivered in response, curling her legs close to her body. "Um, sorry," I said, not expecting it to affect her that much, and she nodded in reply. Considering she was a grandmother, she was acting awfully childlike.

Coming to her feet, she placed her right hand on my side. "You just used an ability that's known as 'concealing eyes.' When you use that, you can make both yourself and nearly anything else invisible to other people."

"Oh...? Wait, *I* used that? When?!"

"Just now, like I said. Just using that unconsciously...It's so much like how I used to be," she said as she brought a hand to her forehead and sighed.

I used a "power"? What is she talking about? All I did was sit down and think a little. I didn't say any magic words or wave my hands around or anything.

I must have looked terribly doubtful to Azami, because she said, "Wait one moment" and turned toward the small desk nestled in between the shelves. She rummaged around the drawers a bit before coming back with a small hand mirror. "Here," she said bluntly, pointing it at me. "Do it again."

"Huh? I told you, I'm not using any power..."

She continued to point the mirror at me, lips pouted. My face in the mirror looked extremely irritated. I didn't know how to "do" anything, and how could I, anyway? I thought about protesting again, but her silent pressure finally broke me down.

I closed my eyes, trying to focus on some vague idea. Like before, nothing in particular came up. Just a picture of my sister, the girl swallowed up in here with me.

...Why did I have to think about that? It made me recall everything again. Thinking about her only made me feel sad.

"...Look, Azami, this isn't accomplishing anything. I think you've got the wrong idea or...something..."

I opened my eyes to find Azami grinning at me in a "There, you see?" kind of way. But it was *just* her. The image of an irritated-looking Tsubomi Kido in the mirror was gone—all it showed were the shelves that loomed behind me.

"What the...?!"

"Just as I said, you can use it!" she said, lowering her mirror and giving me a slap on the head with it. It didn't hurt at all, surprisingly.

"Whoa...A-Azami, how do I get back to normal?!"

Before I could finish, an exasperated Azami showed me the mirror again. It was filled with my alarmed expression. "That's how 'concealing eyes' works," she said. "You don't have to be so suspicious of me, you know."

I marveled at this as she went over to prop the table back up. I was invisible just now. Totally. It was enough to surprise Azami, even—that catlike act must've been her searching for me. And the way she ignored me when I protested...

"Hang on, so you can't hear me, either?"

"What're you talking about?" she said as she fixed the desk's position. "Of course not. You could've shouted at the top of your lungs, and I wouldn't hear a thing...as long as you don't touch me."

I swallowed nervously. *These 'concealing eyes'...Powers like these actually exist.* Azami was telling the truth. And while I'd had trouble believing everything at first, she must've been telling the truth about creating this world…

I stood there, stuck dumb, as Azami took a seat and sighed. "By the way, Tsubomi, where did you get that ability? Because I never ran into anyone like that when I was still in the outside world."

"No, I…" I shook my head. "Like I said, I'm just as surprised as you are. I had no idea I was capable of using this."

"Ooogh," Azami groaned, perplexed. I was clearly not giving her the answer she was looking for. It must have been incredibly frustrating.

…And Azami used to be in my world? She talked about absorbing her daughter into this one, so I assumed she must have lived with her family over there…but why was she holed up in here right now? It was a mystery to me.

She sat there for a bit, stewing to herself, then raised her head suddenly to look at me.

"Wh-what…?"

"No, I…I think I've got it," she said, giving herself a few convincing nods as if that would explain anything. I leaned forward, prodding her to continue.

"Like I said," she began, choosing her words carefully, "the Kagerou Daze swallowed you up because you met the conditions I gave it. You were just about to die, right?"

"Yeah, that much is true…I think."

"But this is weird, though. When I brought my family in here, they weren't in any state to walk around and talk to me like you are."

Indeed. She described it as "horrible" a moment ago, and that did make me wonder a little—why was *I* in perfect condition, then?

"I was thinking," Azami continued before I could ask. "Maybe you're uniquely compatible with the 'concealing eyes' skill in some way. You have to be, or else you couldn't use it."

"Compatible…?" I stated blankly.

"I'm not sure how it happened, but essentially, that power is serving as a 'replacement' for your life…You should be glad for it," she said, turning her face downward so I couldn't gauge her expression. It seemed there was a little bit of sadness to her lips.

I thought over what she had said, then realized what she meant. Azami's granddaughter had gained a power that gave her a second lease on life...and then she escaped this world. Which meant that—presumably—I was about to, too.

Suddenly, I felt something heavy squirm in my chest. Something I wanted to spit out, but I couldn't get it to budge at all. An indescribable feeling of guilt that I could never forget.

Azami tilted an eyebrow at my pained expression. My reaction puzzled her, no doubt. Declared dead once, then granted the right to live again—most people would jump for joy at the concept. Even in this world, too, there must have been tons of people who'd want nothing more than another chance at life. Rin among them, I'm sure. She didn't deserve to die in that fire. She'd make so many people so much happier if she were still alive.

...So why was I deemed the "compatible" one?

"Wh-what's wrong?" a concerned-looking Azami asked. "Is leaving this world making you—?"

"I don't want to go," I whispered, stopping Azami dead in her tracks. "What was it you said? 'Concealing eyes'? ...I don't need it. Give it to someone else. I don't want to be resurrected, anyway."

Azami whirled to her feet, worried. "What are you saying? You still look more than young enough to me. Besides...you had a family, too, didn't you?"

Something about her seemed far more human than a lot of the humans I knew on the outside. She had created a world and performed all manner of other superhuman tasks, but everything about her suggested she and I were alike. It was weird...but really, she was a nice person. And I could tell she was looking at me and picturing her own child and grandchild.

I knew I had no business saying what I was about to say. I was being terrible.

"No, I don't. Nothing at all. I killed my own father just before I came here."

I could hear Azami emit a small, soft sound that nevertheless sounded like a scream. Her face was discolored with grief, as if she had been plunged into a deep well of despair. *Really, what makes her so nonhuman, anyway? This person, worrying herself sick over someone she had only just met—people as kind as her are rarer than hen's teeth in the outside world.*

Compared with her, me and my father...we're far more like monsters than she is.

...If anything, it's Azami who deserves to get out. This used to be Azami's power, I guess—it wasn't a matter of being "compatible" or whatever. Then she could get to see her granddaughter again. That'd be far more meaningful than someone like me getting back out.

I had resolved to tell her this, but Azami stopped me just as I opened my mouth.

"...You had to, didn't you?"

The words stabbed deeply into my chest. She approached me, cautiously, and continued.

"You, you must have had some reason for it, didn't you? Killing your father...I mean, you're such a nice person."

She tried to put a hand on my shoulder, I guess in an attempt to soothe me. But no matter the reason, I just couldn't accept it. I audibly slapped her hand back. "I'm not nice at all!" I shouted. "I killed another person! How could...How could you ever understand that?!"

The words echoed a little in the book-lined chamber as I stared her down. It was followed by a small, stony silence.

I wonder what Azami felt—stepping up to reassure someone, only to be snapped at in reply. Nothing about her face indicated fear anymore. Her jet-black hair waved in the air as she watched me, and I could no longer tell what she was thinking.

Then, slowly, Azami opened her mouth. I turned my eyes away from her face, unable to stand it anymore. She could say pretty much anything right now, I thought. *If she tells me to leave...I will.*

I closed my eyes, waiting for it, only to be taken by an oddly nostalgic feeling from the top of my head. It was something I thought I'd never feel again, and it made my tensed-up body relax.

"...You must have been scared. Alone. I used to be like you—afraid, running wild. I killed...many times."

Her palm gracefully caressed my head. I couldn't respond, trying too hard to hide my own rushing emotions. I didn't know if she knew that or not.

"It was my husband and my daughter who saved me. And I think you'll find someone soon who'll be your own savior. That's why..."

She brought her head closer to mine.

"...I want you to live. Don't choose death for yourself. That's just foolish."

"Then...Then I want you to come with me, Azami. I...I can't put up with these horrible memories by myself...!"

Azami gave me an apologetic look.

Oh, what am I even *saying* now? I never acted like such a spoiled brat to my own mother, even. I knew she couldn't. If she could, she would've left long ago. But after thinking for a moment, she said, "Look this way," stared at me, and fell silent.

The moment she did, every hair on my body stood on end. The mere act of her looking at me suddenly made the entire atmosphere change. Her eyes, red as pomegranates, were imbued with enough force to absorb everything they gazed upon. It wasn't fear, exactly. It was the first time I felt that way in my life. A kind of frightened awe, I suppose. It was hard to so much as lift a finger.

"I am going to use the lone ability I still have with me. Once I do, I'll be able to convey to you all the thoughts, all the emotions I cannot put into words. I will show you how to truly use your 'concealing' skill."

I couldn't reply nor even nod. It was like my body had been turned to stone. Azami showed me an expression I had never seen from her before—one of a sad loneliness.

"The power to 'conceal' works on memories as well. It can envelop and cover all of them—even the saddest and most unbearable memories that have eaten into your mind. I want you to forget those memories...Forget about me and live a happy life."

I struggled to open my mouth. This was probably the end. I had to get at least one word out before then...

"...Ah. And if you run into my granddaughter in the outside world...I hope you'll befriend her."

Come on. Convey this feeling. Put it into words...

"...All right. I promise."

At the very end, Azami quietly nodded, the tears welling in her red eyes.

"...'Projecting eyes.'"

CHILDREN RECORD SIDE -NO. 1- (3)

My consciousness faded, tears flowing out both my eyes as I suddenly remembered everything.

I couldn't see anything. I no longer had my own voice.
It was too late to remember it all, but I knew the words would come.
Then I opened my mouth. I needed to transmit my thoughts, my will.

"Marie, can you hear me?

"You've got a special power.

"My friend told me about it long ago.

"You need to say the name.

"I know she'll save us all.

"Marie, I'm sorry I can't be there with you.

"…Take care of everyone for me."

Right at the very end, on the far end of my long-gone consciousness, I heard the words ring clear.

"Bring it on, Kagerou Daze!"

REAPER RECORD V

…What are those glowing, cubelike things?

I took my eyes off the spot for just a moment, and yet again I was greeted with some crazy new object. It was just the same as before. This world was such a pain in the ass.

Looking at the glowing boxes in front of me, I spotted a man standing in front of them, dressed in outrageous-looking clothing. He looked at my face; then his eyebrows arched up in surprise. He looked human, but I could already tell—those were the "clearing eyes."

There was a person sprawled out by my feet. He had grown a lot, but I could tell who he was right off, too. But…dead? Really? How was he supposed to see anything in the shape he was in? What an idiot.

The blood flowed in an onrush across my body, almost boiling in my veins.

The feeling bursting out of my chest…I suppose "rage" described it best.

I didn't know how long I could remain alive in my granddaughter's body…but that was no real problem. I was, after all, a monster. Reason didn't apply to me.

"Don't make me deviate from my script, you bastard," yelped the inscrutable sight before me.

Who the hell does he think he's talking to?

Trying to take me on…He must have known how pointless that was, no matter how many times the earth had spun around.

"Don't worry. You've spun that ridiculous tale for far too long…"

"…I'm ending it all right now."

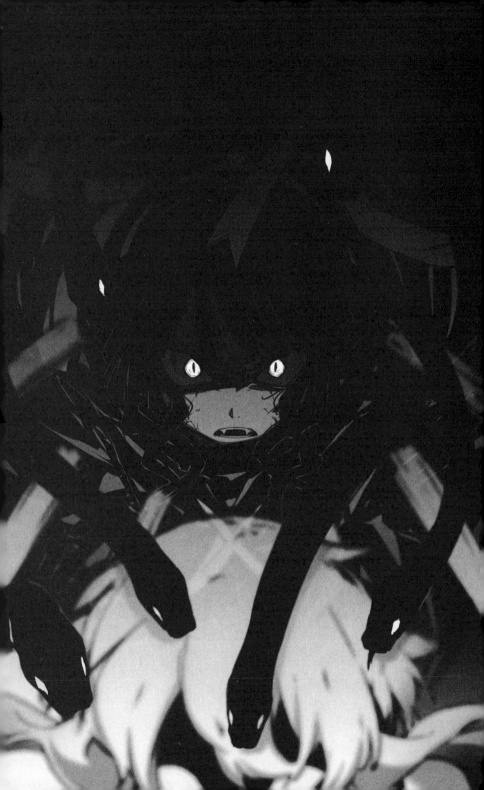

"…And that's seriously gonna work? Hey, uh, just in case it's not clear yet, I definitely don't trust you, so…"

"Huh? Hmm…I dunno. Depends on whether we can reach out to Azami's feelings or not, I guess."

"Yeah…Well, whatever. She's pretty well beyond help anyway."

"Oh, don't say that! I know we can save her. She made a promise."

"…Who can say, really?"

"Ha-ha! Aw, c'mon. Trust me for a change."

"…I'll think about it."

"Great…Well, I better get going."

"Huh? Get going where?"

"Hmm? Well…"

"Off to someone I consider my hero."

AFTERWORD

Kicking Sand in Your Eyes

JIN here. I know it's been a little while, but hey. Thanks for waiting over a year for me after Volume VI—the next volume is finally here, and I put everything I have into it.

Man oh man, has a lot been going on in the past year. I lost my home; some of the staff left...It's been a giant panic party, if you will. It hasn't exactly been a ball all the time, but...
Huh?
Ball? Balls? Big swingin' balls?
(grins)

Anyway, how did you like *Kagerou Daze VII -From the Darkness-*? This volume focuses mainly on everyone's favorite boss, ol' Kido herself, and—no need to mince words here—in the entire history of *Kagerou Daze*, she was the most hellish character to write from a subjective point of view. Haruka in the previous volume was pretty challenging, too, making me wail "Ahhh, Haruka, why do you have to be such a pure-minded bastard?" as I typed away, but this was even harder than that. Like, seriously.

Tsubomi in her younger years is different from me both in gender and in age, so I had very little to go on in terms of understanding her feelings. It was tough, but I can't exactly hop over to the local elementary school to figure out how little girls tick, either. Not if I don't want some police company in short order.

Thus, you had the awesome sight of a twenty-five-year-old man (occupation: unknown) sitting night after night, muttering "Come on, Tsubomiiii, tell me what you're thinking already" as he toiled endlessly at the creative process. That's Tsubomi Kido. Exciting stuff, isn't it?

The *Kagerou Daze* novel story is finally at the final act. I can't say for sure until I start writing it, to be honest, but I'm thinking that the next volume will be the last.

Hard to believe that it's already been four years since this project kicked off, isn't it? I've made it this far mainly thanks to all the fellow staffers carrying me on, to say nothing of all the people reading this. I'm so packed with thankfulness, my nipples are practically erect with it (a hard act to keep up for four years).

To be honest, I'm really torn right now figuring out how the final volume will be structured. I basically have two scenarios in mind that I consider to be the "correct" way to end this. There's a theme I've been trying to bring across during this story, too, and I'm not sure which way is best to express that at the very end.

At the very least, I'm pretty sure the kids who appear in the story will be faced with a pretty big decision. I hope you'll all be looking forward to it. I've been working on my abs a lot lately in order to live up to all your expectations. (Writing? Psh.)

By the way, *Kagerou Daze* will be making a sort of theatrical debut this winter. It's something called an "attraction movie," the sort of thing where your seat rumbles and stuff while you watch the film. Really neat. I can't wait to see it, but the semicircular canals in my ears are just as weak as they are in the characters that appear in the movie. I'm not sure my sense of balance will let me survive the entire showing.

It took just one attraction ride during a trip to the theme park the other day to get me barfing (sadly). While the friends I went with were enjoying the day, I had to sit on a bench and watch a bunch of costumed characters perform onstage. I'll never forget that day.

I do hear, however, that the theater setup is adjusted, so it'll be easy on people who get quickly nauseated by that sort of thing. Even if that describes you, I hope you'll see it if you have the chance. I'll be joining you.

Anyway, this afterword went by surprisingly fast. It's almost over now, in fact.

This was another challenging volume to write, but the more work you put into a story, the more you can't help but love it. Tsubomi was greatly affected in this volume by Rin and Azami—two women with flower-inspired names. It makes me wonder how the rest of the gang see her, now that she's grown up and in full bloom—and how that comes across to you, the reader, for that matter.

The next volume, too, will have its own protagonist. A rather awkward one, and one who I think is supremely deserving of having the "hero" role when it's all said and done. It might be down to the wire for this group of kids' battle against the Kagerou Daze, but who can say how it'll turn out?

I sure can't wait to see. (What? I have to write it first? Psh.)

I'm getting the feeling that I'm being too serious with this afterword. I feel like I'm trying to wrap it up a little too nicely and neatly. That's crazy! What am I doing?! This cannot stand!

Balls, balls, balls, balls, balls!!

There we go. Mission accomplished.
See you all in the next volume!

JIN (Shizen no Teki-P)

Cover Illustration Sketch

Frontispiece Sketch

Illustration 1 Sketch

Illustration 2 Sketch

Illustration 3 Sketch

Illustration 4 Sketch

Illustration 5 Sketch

Illustration 6 Sketch

Illustration 7 Sketch

HAVE YOU BEEN TURNED ON TO LIGHT NOVELS YET?

IN STORES NOW!

SWORD ART ONLINE, VOL. 1–10
SWORD ART ONLINE, PROGRESSIVE 1–4

The chart-topping light novel series that spawned the explosively popular anime and manga adaptations!

MANGA ADAPTATION AVAILABLE NOW!

SWORD ART ONLINE © Reki Kawahara ILLUSTRATION: abec
KADOKAWA CORPORATION ASCII MEDIA WORKS

ACCEL WORLD, VOL. 1–10

Prepare to accelerate with an action-packed cyber-thriller from the bestselling author of *Sword Art Online*.

MANGA ADAPTATION AVAILABLE NOW!

ACCEL WORLD © Reki Kawahara ILLUSTRATION: HIMA
KADOKAWA CORPORATION ASCII MEDIA WORKS

SPICE AND WOLF, VOL. 1–18

A disgruntled goddess joins a traveling merchant in this light novel series that inspired the *New York Times* bestselling manga.

MANGA ADAPTATION AVAILABLE NOW!

SPICE AND WOLF © Isuna Hasekura ILLUSTRATION: Jyuu Ayakura
KADOKAWA CORPORATION ASCII MEDIA WORKS

IS IT WRONG TO TRY TO PICK UP GIRLS IN A DUNGEON?, VOL. 1–8

A would-be hero turns damsel in distress in this hilarious send-up of sword-and-sorcery tropes.

MANGA ADAPTATION AVAILABLE NOW!

Is It Wrong to Try to Pick Up Girls in a Dungeon? © Fujino Omori / SB Creative Corp.

FUJINO OMORI
ILLUSTRATION BY SUZUHITO YASUDA

ANOTHER

The spine-chilling horror novel that took Japan by storm is now available in print for the first time in English—in a gorgeous hardcover edition.

MANGA ADAPTATION AVAILABLE NOW!

Another © Yukito Ayatsuji 2009/ KADOKAWA CORPORATION, Tokyo

A CERTAIN MAGICAL INDEX, VOL. 1–11

Science and magic collide as Japan's most popular light novel franchise makes its English-language debut.

MANGA ADAPTATION AVAILABLE NOW!

A CERTAIN MAGICAL INDEX © Kazuma Kamachi
ILLUSTRATION: Kiyotaka Haimura
KADOKAWA CORPORATION ASCII MEDIA WORKS

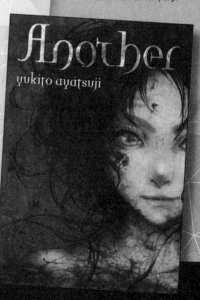

VISIT YENPRESS.COM TO CHECK OUT ALL THE TITLES IN OUR NEW LIGHT NOVEL INITIATIVE AND...

GET YOUR YEN ON!

www.YenPress.com